Nick of Time

a novel by

Anne Lindbergh

Little, Brown and Company
Boston   New York   Toronto   London

First Edition

Library of Congress Cataloging-in-Publication Data

Lindbergh, Anne.
    Nick of time / by Anne Lindbergh. — 1st ed.
        p.   cm.
    Summary: Thirteen-year-old Jericho, whose father runs an unconventional school in their home, passes through an invisible gateway into the year 2094 and discovers a future world of uniformity and overpopulation, where his school has been made a national monument.
    ISBN 0-316-52629-0
    [1. Time travel — Fiction.   2. Schools — Fiction.   3. Science fiction.]   I. Title.
PZ7.L6572Ni   1994
[Fic.] — dc20   93-20777

10 9 8 7 6 5 4 3 2 1

HC

Published simultaneously in Canada by Little, Brown & Company (Canada) Limited

Printed in the United States of America

For Ned—No Blame

1 ❦ Questions and Answers

"Where is Alison?"

That's what I'm hearing all day, every day. Nag, nag, nag.

"Where did she go?" they* keep asking. "What do you mean, you have no idea? You were her best friend, weren't you?"

Yes, I was. And yes, I know where she is. And no, I'm not telling.

So why am I writing this? One thing is sure: it's no true confession that I plan to hand over to the authorities. My plan is to carry on with the lies until they get tired of asking me. But there ought to be a record of the truth in case someday in the future, some kid wants to know. A kid like me, maybe. Or a kid like Nick.

---

* I hate stories that sneak in a lot of information you never asked for, so I'm using footnotes. That way, you can choose whether to be informed or not. For starters, *they* consists of my father, Alison's mom, and Sergeant Mervyn DeSoto of the Alcott police department—in other words, grown-ups.

2 ❦ Nick

The first time I saw him, I thought he was Alison. Seriously. Even though that particular Sunday morning,* only my family was left in the school. But there he stood with his back to me in the kitchen, right where Alison kept the fruit flies for her science project. He was the same height as Alison. Skinny like her, too—wearing jeans and a navy sweatshirt, blond hair tied back in a ponytail. Blond hair like Alison. So how was I to know?

"What are *you* doing here?" I asked.

Then he turned and I saw that he was a boy, which put me against him at the time. Nothing personal—I'm a boy, too. I was just disappointed that he wasn't Alison.

"So what are you *doing* here?" I repeated.

"I'm Nick," he said, as if that explained everything. "Why the flies?"

I said, "They're drosophila."

His expression was serious when he looked into one of the glass culture vials. Respectful, even. Nick had manners. But I'm a noticing person, and I noticed the corners of his mouth twitch.

"What's so funny?" I demanded. "Alison is doing a science project on the patterns of heredity."

"In the kitchen?"

* The first one in November 1994.

I had been through this before with visitors. "We don't believe in classrooms here," I informed him. "We learn in a home environment. *My* home, actually."

"That's terminal!" he said.

"Terminal? You mean lethal?"

He shook his head. "I mean, that's cool. But what can you learn from flies in your kitchen?"

I took a deep breath and started to explain about drosophila. How you mate the wild types with the mutant types and write down which traits appear in the second generation. If you get a second generation, that is—Alison's fruit flies weren't cooperating. Not that she had put much effort into her project so far. She'd been too nervous about the weekend, when she was taking the bus to meet her mom in Boston. Alison's mom happens to be terminal, too. And *I do* mean lethal. Wait and see.

Nick interrupted. "Wait a moment! Are you trying to tell me this is a school?"

"If you didn't know that, why are you here?"

"I thought it was a home. A traditional, old-fashioned single-family home. Built way back in 1986 to house a married couple, eight children, a cook, and a butler. It's all in the tour guide's lecture."

It occurred to me that he had a screw loose. "What tour guide? What are you talking about?"

Instead of answering, he reached for the vial marked FEMALES and spilled the flies out on the breadboard. Most of them were belly up. One crawled away.

"They were all males," he said.

"You might want to explain that to Alison," I suggested. "Like, you know, it was *her* project."

Embarrassment flashed briefly across Nick's face, and he did a curious thing: raising a clenched fist, he gently tapped his forehead several times. "No blame," he said.

I said, "Huh?"

"No blame," he repeated. "When is her project due?"

"Tomorrow. Only it's hopeless if the flies are dead."

"Tell Alison not to worry," he said. "Some kids are doing the same experiment in my school back home. Tell her I'll get some flies for her."

Then he backed against the wall and disappeared.*

---

* One weird detail: he wasn't wearing shoes. Just socks.

3 ❧ Alison

You already know what Alison looked like from behind. But turn her around and she didn't look at all like Nick. His eyes were brown, while hers were blue. His features were rounded, while hers were sharp. I thought she was beautiful, but when I told her so, she'd laugh and say, "You're in love with me.* Your opinion doesn't count."

So what? She was also my best friend. We'd been best friends since she joined the school five years ago. Back then, she and I were the only juniors, and she slept in my room. Eight is young for boarding school, but she was never homesick. Not that she had a home to be sick for, since her mom traveled all year on business. Curious to know what business? A nationwide chain of teen beauty parlors called Curly Girl. You've probably got a Curly Girl in the nearest mall, so you know what I'm talking about. Alison's mom used to run one in Alcott, New Hampshire, five miles down the road. But after dumping Alison at Mending Wall, she started calling herself a consultant and switched to running the people who ran other Curly Girls. On her rare visits to Alcott, she stayed at the Maple Leaf Motel, but she preferred Alison to meet her at her latest

---

* True. Not only that, but I had the hots for her. They weren't shared. Whenever I tried anything, she said, "Forget it, Jericho—I'm strictly a hands-off experience."

job. And no, Alison didn't have a dad she could live with instead. She didn't even know her dad's name. Alison's mom just happened to be single when she had Alison.

So what was special about Alison? Well, like I told her, she was beautiful. Not the ditzy beauty you pay for at Curly Girl, but the natural kind. Plus she used to be happy, and you couldn't hang out with her without feeling happy, too. But her happiness wore off as she grew older until she wasn't happy around people anymore, only animals. She was crazy about animals—especially farm ones. She once told me that she'd gladly trade her mother for a cow. Don't be shocked. With a mother like hers, you would, too.

What else? Not much, just random things. Like her most prized possession was an old Fisher-Price farm she kept set up in her room at school. She was physically standoffish, but I happen to know that she read the Sex Ed textbook on the sly. Oh, and except for her goat milk yogurt, she was a lousy cook. This counts against you in our school, for reasons that I'll explain later. First I'd better explain about the school.

4 ❧ Mending Wall School

Nick's tour guide got one thing right: the house was built in 1986. Otherwise it was a bunch of baloney. My father is single, for starters. I have a sister, but the other six kids are students. The so-called cook and butler are mentors, and as I told Nick, this is a school. "Traditional" is where he really slipped up. Mending Wall is not traditional, as Fugleman keeps reminding us during talkfest. Instead of the three R's, to give you an example, it teaches the three C's.

"Slow down!" you're saying. "Mentors? Talkfest? The three *whats?*"

They say it pays to increase your word power, so here's your chance to get rich:

1. The name of our school comes from a poem by Robert Frost with a line that goes "Good fences make good neighbors." According to my father, a Mending Wall education will help you gather all the rocks in your head and pile them up so the rest of the world has to stay on either one side or the other. If you're not sure how good that is, read the poem.

2. *Fugleman* is my father's title. In German, it means some kind of leader. Why doesn't he want to be headmaster or principal? Because *head-*

master sounds like someone who's out to control your mind, and *principal* means first in importance. But my father claims that his students come first in importance, and he would never dream of controlling their minds. Ho, ho, ho.

3. *Teacher* is a dirty word, too, at Mending Wall. Cathleen and Douglas feel uncomfortable with it. They prefer *mentor,* meaning a trusted counselor. Ho, ho, ho again. Calling the mentors by their first names is part of the Mending Wall experience, by the way. I can handle that, but I've never gotten used to calling my father Fugleman.

4. *Talkfest* is just our name for what most schools call assembly.

5. The three C's stand for cognizance, culture, and conscience. If you want to know what any of those mean, look in the dictionary. Don't be too impressed, though—basically, they add up to the usual stuff you have to learn in school.

So how did all this come about? It began eight years ago when my mother gave birth to my sister, Maple,* handed her to my father, and walked out the door, never to return. She's not about to make an appearance, in case you're wondering—this is our story, not hers.

---

* My father named my sister after a girl in another poem by Robert Frost. Don't bother reading it to find out why that girl was called Maple. Robert Frost didn't know either.

Did my father rant and rave? Only briefly. Did he become embittered and cynical? Forget it! He packed us up and moved to Alcott, New Hampshire, to start the school of his dreams. He had it built from scratch, with an eye to making it look like a home, not an institution.

His original idea was for six kids at the formative stage of their life* to live with us for four whole years and learn everything as a family instead of being in separate grades. He didn't want any classrooms. No dormitories either, just bedrooms. After the first six graduated and went on to high school, he planned to recruit six more. Believe it or not, he expected these kids to live with us nonstop during their Mending Wall experience, so as to avoid contamination by the outside world. That's not quite the way it happened, though. Their parents objected, so he had to change his mind and let them go home for weekends and vacations.

Another thing he changed his mind about was the formative stage. By the time I got to be a little older, it occurred to him that I needed forming, too, and he'd better not wait until I was eleven. That's when he recruited Alison and started a lower school consisting of two juniors. He also made a rule that each senior had to teach each junior one new and interesting thing each day. Luckily for Alison, she adored Mending Wall. Why luckily? Because she hardly ever went home. Like I said, a motel was the only home she had to go to.

When Alison and I grew up to be seniors, we were joined by four new recruits: Jessica, Jason, Bunny, and BVD. By that time, Maple was old enough to be a junior, and she was

---

* Age eleven through age fourteen, according to my father.

joined by Cathleen's daughter, Zoë. Zoë is the only kid at
Mending Wall who doesn't board. She lives with Cathleen
in town, next door to the Grand Union supermarket.

Cathleen is a mentor, remember? There's not much I can
say about her except she's a nice person. That's all anybody
ever says about her: "Cathleen is such a nice person!" Well,
they're right. She wears an I-aim-to-please expression on
her face twenty-four hours a day, which gives her kind of a
doggy look. When we were juniors, Alison used to say, "If
Cathleen had a tail, she'd wag it." She meant it as a compli-
ment, but I've grown a little tired of Cathleen's niceness. If
I were a dog, I'd rather be the kind that bites.

Outside of school hours, Cathleen works as a cashier at
the Grand Union. At Mending Wall, she teaches science,
Native American history, senior math, and Creative Repairs.* Fugleman teaches every other kind of history, plus
ethics and French. Douglas does language arts and junior
math.

Want an instant portrait of Douglas? He wears a moustache—and a sad, sad look on his face when you disappoint
him. He's a plumber in his spare time. If you've leapt to the
conclusion that Mending Wall mentors don't get paid much,
you leapt right. They don't even get room and board. Douglas still lives with his mother at age thirty-three. There's a
rumor going around school that he's having a passionate

---

* This is one of Mending Wall's best courses. You learn where the fuse
  box is, and the valve to shut if a toilet starts overflowing. Plus things
  like the Heimlich maneuver, stress management, and how to change
  the oil in your car.

affair with Cathleen, who is divorced, but I'm afraid it isn't true. They're both too nice.

What more can I tell you about Mending Wall School? It has a rural campus, for one thing. Fugleman keeps reminding us how *campus* means field in Latin. Well, our campus actually *is* a field. We play soccer* on it. There's a brook at the lower end with cedars growing along the banks. Beyond the brook, there are more fields as far as the eye can see. They belong to a farmer named Floyd, who keeps cows on them, and they're really pretty. The whole place is pretty, even the house until you go inside. Inside it's 100 percent school, no matter how hard Fugleman tries to disguise it. How could Nick's tour guide have made such a gross mistake?

Two more details. You're probably wondering about sleeping arrangements, but they're nothing special. Mending Wall is traditional when it comes to roommates. Fugleman moved Alison out of my room once we were seniors and put her with Bunny and Jessica. I got BVD—a kid from Maine who writes a lot of poetry. Jason snores, so he got a single. The second question in your mind is about Alcott, New Hampshire. Where is it? you're asking yourself. Can I get my mom and dad to take me there next time we drive through scenic New England? Here's my answer: wait until you finish this story before you decide if you want

---

* You'll hear more about the Mending Wall soccer team later. For now, all I'll say is that the field slopes. Fugleman says it doesn't matter since we keep switching sides, but visiting teams object. They also object to the dead elm in front of the uphill goal, and to our goats. Why do they keep visiting? Three reasons: they win and win and win.

to come here or not. Then maybe I'll tell. Meanwhile, all you need to know is that everyone in Alcott thinks everyone at Mending Wall is certifiable.* Who knows? They may be right.

---

* Cracked, crazy, cuckoo. Balmy, batty, bonkers. *Non compos mentis.* Use your thesaurus for a change—it's more fun.

5 ❦ Jericho

If you don't know yet that I'm Jericho, you haven't been reading the footnotes.

I'm an average student, fairly sociable, and good enough at sports not to embarrass my friends and family. As for looks, Alison used to rate me six on a scale of ten. She said that was an improvement on the other senior males, which isn't saying much. BVD* was born with a receding chin, and all Jason has going for him is a commercial haircut. Fugleman, believe it or not, still pops a bowl over my head and cuts around it. I'd like to grow my hair and wear it in a braid, but he vetoed the idea. He says that if Mending Wall students put as much effort into being unconventional on the inside as they put into being unconventional on the outside, he'd have a school full of geniuses. Ho, ho, ho.

Reading over that last paragraph, I realize that it makes me sound mediocre. Mediocre I'm not. In many areas, I'm what you might call outstanding. For instance, we don't have grades at Mending Wall, but if there were grades for patience and tact, I'd make the honor roll. I give people the

---

* Don't kid yourself into thinking everybody here rates a chapter. Mostly they get footnotes. This is BVD's. My roommate's full name is Bartolomeo Vanzetti Dunbar. You can find that in the dictionary, too, minus the Dunbar. He writes weird poetry, but he makes great pasta. We get on okay.

benefit of the doubt, and I'm recklessly loyal to my friends.* I should add that I scored the only goal last year out of all the times that Mending Wall played Alcott Middle School. It was an accident, but it still counts.

Alison once wrote down the five things she admired most in me:

1. I use long words.
2. I have a cute, lopsided smile.
3. I'm nice to my little sister.
4. I never look at the Kleenex after I blow my nose.
5. I stay cool.

I tried to make her revise that list, but she wouldn't budge. All I can say is, she was right about staying cool. Anyone else would have freaked out when Nick did his disappearing act in the kitchen. He did it again on Monday.

---

* So is Maple, as you'll see in the next chapter.

6 ❦ Monday

Mending Wall School is a zoo on Mondays. Not just because the kids turn up again, contaminated by the outside
world, but also because Monday talkfest is reserved for
show-and-tell. You may think we're a little old for this, but
at Mending Wall, the concept takes on new dimensions.

Most of the stuff kids bring to show-and-tell is high-tech
and made of plastic. Unfortunately for Zoë, Cathleen is ag-
gressively low-tech and won't let anything plastic into her
home, so Zoë is hard put to think of anything to bring. The
Monday following Nick's visit, she brought a cockroach.

Why did the roach cause an uproar? Maple ate it. No
kidding. She did it out of reckless loyalty to Zoë, who happens to be her best friend. I was with her in the mud room*
at the time, so I can give you a blow-by-blow account.

---

* If you don't know about mud rooms, you've never been north of the
  Big Apple. They serve as decompression chambers between outdoors
  and indoors. Not just in mud season—all year long. Mending Wall
  has a front entrance, too, but it's used so seldom that we forget it's
  there.

TIME: 8:00 A.M.

PLACE: The mud room

After a long weekend in each other's company, Maple and Jericho are impatiently waiting for their friends to arrive. The mud room door opens. Enter Zoë and Jessica. Maple's face lights up; Jericho tries to hide his disappointment.

Jessica: Hey, guys! Check out what I brought for talk-fest: my mom's electric tweezers.

Maple: Big deal. What did you bring, Zoë?

Zoë: A cockroach.

Jessica: Oooh, gross!

Maple: He's cute, Zoë. Where did you get him?

Zoë: Under our kitchen sink. I'm going to tell how roaches date back to dinosaur days and could survive a nuclear holocaust.

Jessica: My mom says if you've got roaches, it means you're living dirty.

Maple: Your mom doesn't know diddly-squat. Roaches are clean. They keep the germs away. Some people even eat them instead of vitamins.

Jessica: Let's see you eat one, then.

Maple: Got any salt?

Jericho: Hey, wait a minute, Maple!

Enter Alison. I noticed right away that she had been crying because her eyes always changed to aqua when she cried. That morning her eyelids were aqua, too, so I guessed that her mother had been trying to turn her into a Curly Girl again. Anyone less like a Curly Girl* than Alison, you cannot imagine. In my concern for her, I forgot to prevent my sister from eating the roach. Instead, I dragged Alison into the kitchen, which I thought was empty at the time.

"What's wrong?" I asked.

"Nothing," said Alison.

I started to hug her, but she backed away. "Forget it, Jericho. I'm strictly a hands-off experience."

"Okay, okay," I said. "Still, if you're wearing makeup, something's wrong."

Alison shrugged and handed me an unsealed, fern-scented pale green envelope. It was addressed to Fugleman, and I didn't have to ask who it was from. Only Alison's mom would write on stationery like that.

"It's for Fugleman," I objected.

"Read it anyway," Alison said. "Go on."

The note inside was dated Sunday, November 6. It informed my father that Alison's mom was about to marry a man named Stanley Mifflin. "Tie the knot" was the exact phrase. Alison's mom claimed that Alison was "tickled pink." Again the exact phrase.

I looked up from the note. "Are you tickled pink?"

Alison muttered a four-letter word.

---

* If you've seen the TV commercial, you know what I mean. The ideal Curly Girl has a color-coordinated lifestyle. Like there's no way she'd keep an old Fisher-Price farm unless it happened to match her eye shadow.

The note went on to say that Stanley Mifflin lived in Mobile, Alabama, where Alison should be sent* on Saturday, November 19. It also said that if Fugleman bought the ticket, he'd be reimbursed. Yeah, sure! I happened to know that Alison's mom still owed him a year's tuition.

"Why doesn't your mom tell Fugleman herself?" I asked.

"I don't know. I guess she's too busy planning for the move to Alabama," Alison said drearily. "Do you realize that November twentieth is my birthday? When I wake up on my fourteenth birthday, there won't be one single thing I like about my life, starting with the way I look."

I made a sympathetic face. "That sucks! But what's wrong with the way you look?"

"Call me on November twentieth, and I'll give you the gory details. Mom is opening a Curly Girl in Mobile, and she wants me to advertise it on TV. Me personally. She's convinced that with a complete makeover, I'd be the perfect Curly Girl. So that's what I'm getting as a birthday present, like it or not: facial, haircut, body wave."

"You don't have to let them touch your body," I said. "Just say no."

"It's my hair that gets the body wave, moron. And she even wants me to take courses at a charm school."

"Just say no," I repeated. "You're good at saying no, aren't you?"

"Only here at Mending Wall. When I'm with her, I turn to mush. I don't know how it happens, but I start giving in and agreeing to everything she says. I even agreed to practice wearing makeup, starting yesterday."

* Airmail.

Alison began to cry. I slipped a comforting arm around her waist, but she slipped it off again. Hitching herself up on the counter next to her science project, she reached for one of the glass culture vials. "Jericho!" she gasped, changing the subject. "Check out my drosophila!"

I did. That vial was empty the last time I saw it. The one live fruit fly had crawled away, remember? But now there were a bunch of weird-looking things swarming around in there. They were too big to be drosophila, and they were every color of the rainbow. I guessed what had happened.

"Holy Moses!" I said.* "They're terminal!"

"Terminal?"

"New word," I explained. "Nick must have brought these, but he goofed. They're not fruit flies, Alison."

Alison didn't agree. She got all excited and explained how her original flies had laid eggs, and she had developed a mutant strain, and her name would go down in history.

"There's just one problem," I warned her. "Nick said your fruit flies were males, and males don't lay eggs."

"Who the heck is Nick?"

I didn't answer because all of a sudden, he was there, next to the place on the wall where Fugleman marks our heights twice a year, to see how we grow.** He was dressed

---

* That's not what I really said. I'm keeping a lot of the words I really said out of this story, in case they'd be the cause of some parent or teacher not letting you read it.

** He measures us in September and again in June. The top of Nick's head came exactly to the line marked Alison, 9/94. Also Jericho, 9/94, and Bunny, 9/94. The girls had been taller than me for a couple of years, but I caught up.

the same as the day before: hair tied back, navy sweatshirt, and jeans. No shoes, just socks. Alison seemed kind of stunned.

"They were males," said Nick. "All males and all dead except for one. Your friend was right."

He had an odd way of talking: pleasant but bland, without any character to his voice. Alison stared at him as if he were a ghost.

"But *you* were right about the mutant strain," Nick reassured her. "They're called Perrin's drosophila, and they were developed in 2013—I found out for you."

"You're crazy," Alison said. "You mean 1913 or some other date in the past."

"That *is* in the past," said Nick.

The bell rang. Not an electric ear-splitter like they have in public schools, but a big copper cowbell that Fugleman keeps in the hall. When he rings it, he means now.

"Crimeny!" said Alison. "I never wrote up my project."

"Write it during break," I suggested. "Perrin's drosophila—I'll jot that down for you."

I scribbled the name on the back of Alison's mom's fern-scented pale green envelope and was just jamming it into my pocket when Nick went out again. Not out the door like any normal kid. What he did was, he backed against the height chart and went out like a candle flame. This time we both saw him do it.*

---

* If you're expecting me to tell you what the roach tasted like, forget it. I didn't ask Maple because I didn't want to know. It sure caused an uproar, though. Plus Cathleen had to find Zoë something else for Show-and-Tell.

7 ❦ Good Fences Make Good Neighbors

Some people think my father is weird.

Correction: some people *know* my father is weird. So what? I'm weird. You're weird. Who cares if at the start of every morning talkfest, every school day in my life, I've had to stand up with seven other kids and say "Good fences make good neighbors"? No, I'm not sure what it means. Do you know what "with liberty and justice for all" means? If so, do you believe it?

But if you ask me, Robert Frost would turn over in his grave. "Mending Wall" is a good poem, and it's too bad that it's been ruined for eight innocent kids in Alcott, New Hampshire.

On that Monday morning, two of the kids didn't even hear what they were saying. They were thinking of a different kind of wall from the one Frost and his neighbor were fixing, stone by stone.

"How did he do it?" Alison whispered, after getting my attention with a jab of her elbow.

"Beats me."

"Do you think he's an alien?"

"Why not? He's sure as heck not from New Hampshire."

Bunny* was standing on my other side. She demanded to be let in on the secret, so I told her that we had just seen a kid go through a wall.

"Did it hurt?" she asked.

Don't get me wrong. I wasn't about to spill the beans to just anyone who came along. But I've discovered that the more incredible a thing is, the more you can tell the truth and get away with it. If you don't believe me, try this:

1. Rob a bank.
2. Go to your parents and say, "Hey, Mom 'n' Dad, I just robbed a bank!"
3. Smile.

I smiled. Bunny smiled. Fugleman said, "Excuse me, Jericho, would it be asking too much to show a little consideration for the speaker?"

The speaker was Zoë. She was holding up the thing that Cathleen had found to replace the roach for show-and-tell. It was shiny and metallic, about three inches long. The top end was welded together. From there on down, it was split in two. The bottom ends—about half an inch apart from each other—were pointed. Three guesses.

"This is a mostly nonpolluting device," Zoë began.

"It looks *totally* nonpolluting to me," said Cathleen.

* A word about Bunny: don't be fooled by her name. It makes her sound cute and innocent, which she's not. In fact, I used to be afraid of her. She's obsessed with equality and, being female, thinks she deserves more of it than any male. Am I still afraid of her? Keep on reading.

Zoë shook her head. "That's because manufacturers hoodwink the public into thinking that what you see is what you get.* You don't see any pollution because it doesn't take any pollution to use it, but it took some pollution to make it. You could make one yourself, though. Out of wood and Scotch tape."

Fugleman frowned. "How would you cut the wood?"

"With a knife, dummy," Zoë said.

"A certain amount of pollution is involved in producing a knife," Fugleman said, ignoring the insult. "A *lot* of pollution is involved in producing Scotch tape."

"Okay, so I'd make it out of twigs and a piece of vine," Zoë told him impatiently.

"What would you use it for?" asked Jessica.

This was a dumb question. Jessica knew at least one use for it because she had just finished explaining how her mom used hers to pull the hairs out of her nose. But Jessica had also just finished boring us to tears with her own contribution to show-and-tell and was aware of the fact.

"Come up here and I'll demonstrate," Zoë offered with an evil smile on her face.

Jessica stood up, but Fugleman made her sit down again. "This presents a challenging dilemma," he said. "The hidden flaw in well-intentioned ecological reasoning. Are more of Earth's resources consumed in our effort to produce nonpolluting tools than to produce their so-called polluting counterparts? Any ideas?"

---

* This is the way we're taught to speak at Mending Wall. I swear! Even eight-year-olds. It's the Fugleman influence.

I glanced around at the other faces. They were blank except for Alison's, which was smeared with makeup. I felt like killing her mom. What right did she have to turn Alison into a Curly Girl and take her out of Mending Wall? After all, the school had been her family for the past five years—a family that liked her the way she was.

"Life sucks!" I said aloud.

"Let's stick to the subject at hand," said Fugleman. "I am declaring an Unscheduled Experimental Unit Day today. Our goal is to find a pollution solution to tweezers."

8 ❧ A Romantic Interlude

"So we'll get married," I tell Alison.

"No."

"Why not?"

"I'm thirteen, you jerk."

"Who cares? A lot of girls get married at thirteen."

"Not to boys of thirteen, they don't."

"I bet in some places they do. Like Mexico. I'll find out and make all the arrangements. You won't have to do anything but marry me."

"No."

"Give me one good reason."

"Who do you know who's happily married? Look me straight in the face and name someone."

When I look her in the face I notice for the first time that the aqua eye shadow has been applied in the form of two small hearts, one on each lid. Somehow I don't think that's what her mom had in mind. It's reassuring, though. It proves Alison isn't about to give in without a fight.

"Let's run away together," I suggest.

"Thanks," says Alison, "but I can do that by myself."

9 ❦ Tweezer Teams

What about Alison's science project? Forget it! Regular classes were cancelled due to the Unscheduled Experimental Unit Day, so Cathleen gave her a week's extension. By that time, the Perrin's drosophila had all dropped dead. But don't worry, Alison wasn't too broken up over it. She had more important matters on her mind.

Right after talkfest, Fugleman paired us up into tweezer teams. Alison got BVD. I got Bunny. An award* was offered to the best pollution solution, and in case you're wondering, it went to Zoë and Maple. All they did was break off a willow twig, bend it around, and fasten the loop with grass. It might have worked okay to pull a hair out of your soup, but for pulling one out of your nose, it was a dead loss.

Bunny and I didn't even get an honorable mention. Why not? Because Bunny kept insisting that recycling was more environmentally correct than using new materials, even if the new materials were twigs and grass. I happened to agree with her, but there was no chance we'd win with rubber bands and plastic picnic knives. Not at Mending Wall.

---

* Fugleman always gives the same award: a gold star next to your name on the height chart on the kitchen wall. I hadn't earned any yet for 9/94. Neither had Bunny or Alison.

We didn't care, though. Like Alison, we had more important matters on our minds.

"Wasn't he wearing a seat belt?" Bunny asked when we were in the kitchen, hunting for the knives.

"Wasn't who wearing a seat belt?"

"You know. The kid who went through the wall. Where did it happen, anyway—out on Route Two?"

"It wasn't a car accident," I said. "Listen, how about using a turkey wishbone? It even looks like tweezers."

Bunny ignored my suggestion. "Bike accident, then. Or are you telling me it was a fight?"

I told her to drop it, but Bunny isn't the dropping type. Once she latches onto a subject, she rarely lets go. Instead, she starts breathing faster and her nose begins to twitch.*

"Who was the kid?"

"Drop it," I repeated. "I was just joking around."

"Yeah, sure."

She stood there watching me expectantly, so after a while I asked, "Do you believe in aliens?"

"Of course," Bunny said.

"Of course? What do you mean, of course? It's a highly controversial subject."

"Sure, but you read about them all the time. You know: 'New Hampshire Schoolteacher Kidnapped by UFO, Gives Birth to Frog'."

"Get real!" I said.

"'Inca Treasure Found on Moon'," she went on glee-

---

* Bunny's nose twitches when she gets upset or excited. It's the only truly rabbity thing about her.

fully. " 'Infra-galactic Alien Attends Town Meeting, Tells All'."

"Get real," I said. "What's 'infra-galactic,' anyway?"

"Search me," said Bunny.

"Can I really?" I asked.

She got down to work on our pollution solution as if she had decided to drop the subject after all. Was I grateful? If you answered yes, I'd better tell you one more thing about Jericho: he's lousy at keeping a secret.

"What would you do if you saw a kid back against a wall—this wall, for instance—and disappear?" I asked.

"I'd look on the other side of the wall," said Bunny.

10 🌷 Kisses and Tootsie Rolls

Houses built as far north as ours is—houses built recently, at least—tend to be well insulated. Our kitchen, for instance, has some room between the inside and the outside walls. Mostly it's filled up with copper pipes and that fluffy pink fiberglass insulation stuff, but there's a crawl space, too, in case you need to go in and fix the plumbing. You get there by removing a panel next to the sink. Bunny and I removed it.

"He's not here," I said after we had crawled through as far as we could get.

She was so close to me that I could feel her shrug in the dark.

"It was a dumb idea," I said.

She shrugged again.

"Girls have the craziest sense of logic!" I complained.

Bunny let her breath out in a hiss. "Justify that statement, Jericho."

"Okay, *some* girls have a crazy sense of logic. According to you, if this alien went through the wall, he has to be somewhere back here with the pipes."

"Not 'has to be.' Might be," said Bunny. "What is scientific research if not the long and tedious process of eliminating a multitude of hypotheses?"

"Who said that?"

"I did."

And she probably did, too. I mean, she wasn't just quoting—it was her own, peculiar thought. I'm not the only one at Mending Wall who uses long words.

I sighed. "Well, back to the pollution solution."

"Not yet," she said with a sudden thrill to her voice. "Look what I found!"

Don't get excited—it wasn't Nick. It was a long-forgotten stash from the Sugar War.* The loose stuff like candy corn was in a sorry state, but the Tootsie Rolls were as good as ever. At least, I assumed they were Tootsie Rolls by the shape and taste. We were in the dark, remember.

"Want a kiss?" Bunny asked.

I said, "Um—"

Then I realized what she meant and said, "No, thanks. I get a bad reaction."

"A Hershey's Kiss," she specified.

"I know. I get zits from chocolate."

"You can get zits from lying, too," she said scornfully. "You thought I was putting the make on you, didn't you?"

"No, I swear!"

"That's a lie, Jerko."**

That's right, she called me Jerko. I felt kind of sick all of

---

* The Sugar War lasted nineteen days in March 1990. It began when Fugleman decided that the Mending Wall students were acting hyper, due to candy consumption. Any student caught consuming was sent home. It ended when he found that this "punishment" stepped up consumption rather than discouraging it. A lot of good stuff was hidden around the school during the Sugar War. Four years later, we're still finding it.

** She was right, but in case you're worried, lying doesn't give me zits.

a sudden, and it wasn't just from candy. So I tried to get out of there, only I was the one who had gone in first, so I had to squeeze by her in order to leave. Which was a mistake because she got really mad. She smelled good, though: a mixture of Tootsie Roll and shampoo.

"Don't get any ideas," she snarled as I paused to take a second sniff.

"Forget it," I said. "Who said I was even tempted? There's only one real girl in this school as far as I'm concerned, and that's Alison."

The snarl left Bunny's voice as she asked, "By the way, what's up with Alison? She looks as if she's been crying her eyes out, and there's all this blue crap on them."

I told her about the fern-scented pale green envelope and Mobile, Alabama. Bunny's eyes flashed when she heard that Alison was being made over into the perfect Curly Girl.

"You're kidding! Alison's mom is truly evil."

"I kid you not. 'Evil' is too strong, though. The fact that Mending Wall girls don't wear makeup doesn't mean that people are evil who do. Let's just say she's lethal."

"People who won't let women be themselves are evil," Bunny said firmly, "and women who want to make other women over are even worse. It's spiritual rape."

I couldn't help grinning. "Spiritual rape? Give me a break! Why do you always have to—"

"Because I'm superior, Jerko," Bunny interrupted. When I burst out laughing, she got mad and took a swipe at me. Luckily, by then we were back out in the kitchen, so I had room to move away.

"I dare you to hit me!" I said, still laughing.

"Keep on laughing and I will."

"Try it and I'll hit you back."

"You wouldn't dare!"

"Oh, yeah? Try me."

We went on like that for a while. I'd laugh, and she'd take a swipe at me, and then she'd laugh and I'd take a swipe at her. Only pretty soon none of the laughter was the funny kind, and things got kind of rough. In fact, the last swipe I took at her made Bunny lose her balance. She stumbled backward against the wall right where the height chart was, and the next thing I knew, she had disappeared.

What could I do? She wasn't my first choice as companion for the adventure of a lifetime, but I could hardly let her go alone. Wherever she'd gone, I felt morally obligated to go, too. So I took a deep breath and followed—except nothing happened. I mean, I kind of sank into the wall, and things went gray for a split second, but my feet hadn't moved an inch.

Bunny was there again, to my relief. Her hair was a little mussed up, but otherwise she was the same old Bunny. And I was the same old Jericho, no doubt about that. The only difference was in the kitchen. It was almost the same, but not quite.

Bunny noticed, too. "Where are we?" she asked.

"Same *where*," I said. "Wrong *when*."

11 ❧ Gold Stars

The first thing to catch my eye was the floor. The kitchen floor at Mending Wall—when the house was a school, I should say—was covered with linoleum in a sunburst pattern that you never saw because of all the scuff marks, spilled food, and scientific experiments. This new floor had been stripped to the original wooden boards, waxed, and buffed. A printed sign next to the door read:

REMINDER
All Outdoor Footwear
Must Be Checked at Ticket Counter
HELP PRESERVE NEW HAMPSHIRE'S
MONUMENTS!

"Monuments?" I whispered.

Bunny rose to her feet and walked cautiously forward. There was no one in the room except us.

"Check out the red velvet ropes, Jericho! Like in a museum. I guess they don't want anyone touching stuff."

I touched one of the ropes, still wondering if this was just a dream. "Do you suppose some kid tampered with those Tootsie Rolls? You know, injected them with acid or something? And we're hallucinating?"

"No," said Bunny. "Look—there's the place where Jason

wrote the four-letter word. You can still read it through the paint.* And hey, come check out my stars!"

I didn't know what she was talking about. I didn't want to know. What I wanted was to go home. If I had to time-travel, why couldn't it have been with Alison?

"What stars?" I muttered. "This place gives me the creeps. Where are the other kids? It feels as if we're all dead."

"I bet we are," Bunny said cheerfully.

She leaned against the rope, rocking the brass stands at either end. I caught one of them just in time. "Are you crazy? Careful!"

"What's your problem?" she asked.

"Someone might hear us. We might get kicked out, and then how would we get home?"

"We *are* home," Bunny reasoned. "You said yourself that we were in the same place, so if anyone has a right to be here, we do. How do you suppose I earned the stars?"

The light finally dawned: she meant the gold award stars on Fugleman's height chart. There were two of them next to Bunny's name and three next to mine. My spirits rose a little; those stars proved that I'd get back to real life again.

"It looks like Alison doesn't earn any at all at five-foot-five,"** said Bunny.

---

* Jason wrote the word with an indelible marker in April 1993. Fugleman made him paint over it, but the paint worked kind of like a highlighter, so people just noticed it more.

** Only Mending Wall would have an award system where your height gets credited, rather than your report card or something logical like that.

"What do you expect?" I asked crossly. "She's leaving a week from Saturday. Let's get out of here. If we get stuck in this place, I may never see her again."

Bunny gave me a sassy look. "What's the big hurry—you chicken or something?"

So I moved closer to the height chart and studied it casually, taking my time. That's how I noticed the new name. Remember when I said how Alison, Bunny, and I were all the same height in 9/94? Well, now there was a fourth name next to ours in big block letters: NICK.

"The nerve of him!" said Bunny.

"I grew, though," I said, pointing higher up to the place marked "Jericho, 6/97." "Looks like I finally got taller than you."

"Says who? My last height marked on here is for June, ninety-six, when I graduated. I probably caught up to you again in high school. What were you doing still at Mending Wall in ninety-seven?"

"I lived here, remember?"

"I bet you flunked. You had to stay back because you were such a lousy cook."

"Are you kidding? Cooking is how I got those stars."*

At the time, it seemed funny to be talking about our future as if it were our past. I gave Bunny a playful shove. She gave me a playful shove. Once we started laughing, we couldn't stop.

Not until a voice behind us said, "Take off your boots!"

---

* It's about time I told you what the deal is with cooking. The seniors take turns making supper as part of the curriculum. My specialty is tuna casserole.

12 ❦ Meanwhile, Back at Mending Wall

Just kidding. I couldn't have cared less what the tweezer teams were up to in our absence. I bet you don't either.

13 ❦ Glen Alcott

Just for the record, I was not wearing boots. Neither was Bunny. We were wearing cleats because Mending Wall was playing Alcott Middle School on Thursday, and if Fugleman hadn't declared the Unscheduled Experimental Unit Day, we would have spent most of the morning at soccer practice. But I could see what the tour guide meant.

That's right—tour guide. There was absolutely no doubt about it. She wore this ludicrous red cap with some kind of badge on the visor, and a red tunic with gold buttons, and iridescent panty hose. She had on felt slippers, but the people with her were padding around in their socks.

"How in the name of blame did you kids get past security?" she demanded.

"Search me," said Bunny.

The tour guide did. She ran her hands up and down Bunny right there in front of the crowd, and felt in all her pockets. Bunny glared, but she kept her mouth shut after that. So did I. We both unlaced our cleats and padded out of the kitchen toward the mud room, where I assumed we'd find the official entrance to the traditional, old-fashioned single-family home.

We assumed right. One side of the mud room had been preserved. Some unfamiliar jackets hung on wooden pegs three feet above the floor with familiar names written over them: Jericho, Jason, Jessica, et cetera. Along the opposite wall, a rack had been constructed. It was full of shoes. There was a ticket counter, too, with a man in charge.

"Welcome to the Fugleman Homestead," the man recited. "Kindly remove your boots and proceed down the east corridor, following the blue stripe on the floor. I believe you'll catch up with our tour guide in the kitchen."

We stared. Why? Because he was wearing makeup. Bunny says so were the men in the crowd, but I hadn't noticed. This man was dressed like the tour guide: red cap, red tunic. I couldn't help leaning over the counter to see if he was wearing panty hose. While I was at it, I grabbed a glossy brochure and crammed it into my pocket. According to the cover, it told about "The Fugleman* Homestead: A Jewel in New Hampshire's Glorious Past."

"Take another," the man offered. "Take several, and pass them around. There's a supplementary insert on Cow Land. And on your way out, don't forget to stop at our souvenir counter."

Another weird thing about him: his voice. Except for being male, it was like the tour guide's voice. Which, except for being more mature, was like Nick's. All three spoke the way moderators do on TV talk shows in our time: uniformly pleasant, no matter what they're saying.**

---

* As I already explained, this is my father's title, not his name. His surname (mine, too) happens to be Betts.

** I found out later that everyone in the United States talked this way. It's because in Nick's time, kids stayed at home through second grade and learned from nationwide programs on TV. All the teachers on these programs were trained to speak the same, so as not to disadvantage any of the kids.

"Would you happen to know a kid named Nick?" I asked.

The man nodded. "He's still in school."

I described him to be sure we meant the same Nick: blond, skinny, dressed in navy blue. The man kept nodding.

"Alcott Middle School?" I asked.

"Glen Alcott Junior High," he corrected me.

"*Glen* Alcott—where's that? How do you get there?"

He waved toward the exit door. "Down the hill, about a quarter of a mile. You ought to know that. Where in the name of blame are you kids from, anyway?"

We were silent for just a little bit too long. Long enough for him to look suspicious. Then Bunny said, "Alcott. We're from Alcott."

"Glen Alcott or Alcott Heights?"

Bunny shook her head. "Just plain Alcott."

"There hasn't been a 'just plain Alcott' since I was a boy," he said pleasantly, as if he were only saying, "We will return after these messages."

A shiver ran through me. "Let's go," I said to Bunny.

She thrust her jaw out stubbornly. "If you mean back the way we came, I'm not ready yet. Let's explore for a while."

So instead of checking our cleats, we laced them up again and walked out into the campus, which hadn't changed much except for the dead elm being gone. We went down to the brook where the cedars grow. Across a little iron bridge, which hadn't been built yet in our time. Through a huge gate with a sign that read:

WELCOME TO SCENIC GLEN ALCOTT
A Nice Place to Live

It was scenic, all right. Block after block of condominiums, where once there had been Floyd's fields. Some scene!

14 ❧ A Nice Place to Live

"Who is Blame?" Bunny wondered.

"What do you mean?"

"'In the name of Blame,' that guy said. The tour guide said it, too."

"Nick said something about blame, the first time I met him," I said, remembering. Then I shrugged. "It probably doesn't mean anything. It's like 'for Pete's sake' or 'for the love of Mike.' Just the way people talk in the future."

"How far in the future?"

"How in the name of blame am I supposed to know?"

We walked on for a while in silence. And when I say silence, I don't mean our own, although we weren't talking much. I mean Glen Alcott was so quiet that we could hear ourselves breathe. It was spooky.

"They're using alternative power, anyway," Bunny said approvingly.

I looked up and saw massive flat constructions on the condo roofs. "Those could be some kind of receptors, like satellite dishes."

"All facing south? I tell you, they've gone solar. And you know what else is different? There are no cars."

She was right. I didn't see a single vehicle—not in the street, not parked, not anywhere. I didn't see any people, either.

"Where is everybody?" I asked. "With so many buildings, there has to be a population."

"Watching TV?" Bunny suggested. "It's ten o'clock: *Mr. Rogers' Neighborhood.*"

"Yeah, sure."

"Mr. Rogers must be dead, though," she added with a giggle. "And Mr. McFeely, and Lady Elaine Fairchild."

I reached for her hand.

"Chicken," she said.

So I dropped it again.

We walked around for about an hour, keeping track of where we turned left or right because the streets and buildings were so much the same. Everything lacked variety. Even the trees, which turned out to be artificial maples installed at regular intervals and equal heights. There was an IGA supermarket every ten blocks, but they were identical. They were also empty. I figured there must be someone in there to keep an eye on things, since they all seemed open for business. But I wasn't about to go in and find out.

Bunny said, "Boring!"

"Maybe that's good," I said.

What I meant was, at least boring isn't dangerous. Still, it was a little disappointing. You'd expect the future to be packed with awesome novelties, but we only noticed two strange things on that first walk through Glen Alcott. One was the window of a clothing store where all the mannequins—male and female—wore tunics.* The other was graffiti. In huge spray-paint curlicues it said: BLAME IS TERMINAL! We never found any school.

So what did we do? We turned back, tracing our steps until we reached the little bridge that crossed to the Mending Wall campus. Or maybe I should say to the Fugleman Homestead. Even Bunny was ready to leave by then.

But it turned out not to be so easy.

---

* Bunny says I should tell you over what, so here goes: over tights, bare legs, or skirts. Yes, even the men. If you think that's weird, look in the encyclopedia under *F*, for fashion. Weird was not invented in the future.

15 ❦ A Word to the Wise

By the way, I'm not chicken. I'm just practical, level-headed, and blessed with an extremely useful sense of self-preservation. Ask anyone.

16 ❦ A Toxic Shock

"Very funny!" Bunny said in an outraged voice.

She took it as a personal insult that the Fugleman Homestead was closed. This didn't surprise me; in case you haven't guessed, Bunny always takes things personally.

"They've got no right!" she grumbled.

The door to the mud room was locked. Also a metal grill that had been installed to reinforce it. A sign informed us that public tours of the monument were conducted hourly from 9:00 to 4:00 on normal days, and noon to 4:00 on observation days.

"Whatever those are," said Bunny.

I shrugged. "Weekends, maybe?"

"It doesn't make sense," she reasoned. "We were just in there. So were a lot of other people, and it was morning. It still is."

"How do you know?"

"Look at the sun, Jerko."

I looked at her instead, and she said, "Sorry. I won't call you that again."*

"Well, let's not panic," I suggested.

Bunny scowled at me. "Who's panicking? I'm depressed, is all. If this is the future, I don't like it."

---

* She said it once more, though. Wait and see.

"Just be glad we don't have to live here, then. We're going home."

"How? You don't expect me to wait around until nine o'clock tomorrow morning, do you?"

"What's the alternative?"

Actually, I had already thought of an alternative myself: my sister's window. Maple's bedroom is on the way up to the second floor. Back in our time, at least, her window had no lock.

"Give me a boost," I told Bunny. "If we can still get in that way, I'll pull you up."

We still could. The window stuck badly, but I finally forced it open and climbed in. I wasn't sure what to expect. Maple's original furniture, perhaps, with a display of her pink plastic barrettes labeled "Hair ornaments, circa 1990." But no.

"Holy Moses!" I said. "Come check this out."

Bunny was as surprised as I was. At what? At your typical teenage boy's room.* Messy. Odorous. Some empty glasses caked with a weird greenish substance. Clothes on the floor. Including a jockstrap, believe it or not. And a bunch of posters on the wall, all of a rock group called Toxic Shock.

I said, "Cool!"

Bunny's nose twitched. "What a dump! Got a pen on you?"

As usual, there was a lot of junk in my pocket. Some of it fell out while I was fishing around inside, so I had to go

* Bunny says that phrase is sexist. Okay, then—the room just happened to be like the one I share with BVD.

chasing after pennies, but I finally found a pencil stub. "What for?" I asked, handing it to Bunny.

"We're going to leave this guy a message from the past," said Bunny.

Standing on tiptoes, she crossed out SHOCK on one of the posters and scribbled some big black letters to spell TOXIC WASTE DISPOSAL AREA!

Then she pried a tack loose from one corner and fastened the jockstrap to an appropriate spot on the guitarist.

"Grow up, Bunny," I said.

She laughed. "I've already grown up. Grown up and passed away again. This is the future, remember?"

I didn't want to remember. Who wants to be reminded that they're dead? Especially by a twitchy-nosed, fight-picking kid named Bunny. More than ever, I wanted to get back to Alison. So I kept a dignified silence as we made our way cautiously down to the kitchen and the height chart on the wall. My mind was working hard, though—thinking up devastating comments. I came up with three good ones,* but I forgot to use them because right before we left, Bunny kissed me on the cheek.

"Thanks for bringing me along," she said. "I had a great time."

My silence lost some dignity when I blushed. Poor old Jericho—suckered again!

---

* You want me to write them down so you can use them on some kid you know, don't you? Forget it—I may need them later.

17 ❧ Irony

It would have been too much to expect to come back to an empty kitchen. Not on a weekday morning. Not when the kitchen is also the science lab. So it came as no surprise that we were seen—by Jessica.

A word about Jessica. I've mentioned her several times already without a whole lot of enthusiasm. I know what you're thinking: back in chapter five, I said how I give people the benefit of the doubt, so what about Jessica? I tried, that's what. I tried really hard to like her, but I couldn't. I also tried not to dislike her, which was easier. Why? Because she's kind of featureless. So is Jason, who happens to be her twin. They're both quiet without being thoughtful. Friendly without being stimulating. You don't mind when they join a group, but you don't miss them when they don't. In other words, they're blah. Or according to Douglas,* good, all-around citizens of Mending Wall. You get to choose.

What was Jessica doing in the kitchen? Looking for Cathleen to take out a splinter. And what did she do when Bunny and I popped out of the wall? She threw up, is what. Poor Cathleen! One problem after another that morning.

* Come to think of it, you haven't heard much about Douglas yet, either. You're in for a treat.

"Gross!" Bunny said, stepping gingerly over the puddle. "What have you been eating, Jessica?"

Jessica was in no condition to answer, but in case you're interested, it was a prune juice popsicle.* She wanted the sticks for her pollution solution and being a good citizen, felt obliged to eat the popsicle part first. After cleaning up the mess, Cathleen felt too queasy to take out the splinter Jessica got from trying to bend the sticks. She made Douglas do it instead. And the only way Douglas could get it out was by using Jessica's mom's electric tweezers. That's irony.

---

* No, you can't buy prune juice popsicles. Are you kidding? I bet your mom asked that, not you. The one Jessica ate was homemade by Cathleen.

18 ❦ Sex

"Wait a minute!" you're protesting. "What about Jessica? Don't tell me she kept her blah little mouth shut?"

Of course not. Even the blah can blab! But remember how I said the more incredible a thing is, the more you can tell the truth and get away with it? While Douglas was taking out her splinter, Jessica told him what she'd seen. Don't worry, Douglas didn't believe her. He didn't believe me, either, when I told the truth. Here's a little scene to prove it:

Douglas: (*Coming up to me in the hall, where I'm chatting with Alison*) Could I have a word with you, Jericho?

Jericho: You've just had eight, Douglas, but I'm good for a few more.

Douglas: (*After a forced chuckle*) Very funny. Uh, Jericho, why was Jessica so upset? What's this I hear about you and Bunny coming out of the wall?

Jericho: That's correct. We heard a noise, and we thought maybe someone was hiding there. So we went into the crawl space, but all we found was a bag of candy. Jessica freaked out when we came back again.

Douglas: (*With a sad, sad look*) Jericho!

Jericho: Okay, okay. Bunny and I were time traveling. You can go back and forth to the future through that wall.

Douglas: (*In a gentle voice*) Please be serious, Jericho. You and Bunny are soon to reach the age of puberty.

Jericho: I don't know about Bunny but personally, I've reached it. Stage two, anyway.*

Douglas: All the more reason to stay out of the crawl space.

Jericho: I don't get it.

Douglas: I think you know what I'm referring to.

Jericho: Oh, you mean *sex!* Don't worry. I wasn't having sex with Bunny in the crawl space. There wasn't room.

Douglas: (*With another sad, sad look*) Jericho!

Jericho: I wasn't even feeling her up. If I wanted to, I wouldn't do it in the crawl space. I'd do it in the sports equipment shed. I don't want to, though. The only girl in this school I want to feel up is Alison.

Alison: Forget it, Jericho—I'm strictly a hands-off experience.

* Alison isn't the only one who reads the Sex Ed textbook.

19 ❦ Enter Fugleman

Alison was no exception to the Jericho Rule of Incredibility. Before I finished telling her about the Fugleman Homestead, she began tapping her foot restlessly.

"Let me get this straight," she interrupted. "There's a way to the future through that height chart on the wall, but it's only ever happened to you and Bunny. Is that what you're trying to say?"

"Nick did it, too, remember. You saw him."

"I don't know," she said, shaking her head slowly. "I don't know what I saw. I mean, every kid in school has backed up against that height chart. Lots of times."

"So you think I'm lying?"

She gave me a puzzled look. "The problem is, it's not like either of you to make up that kind of story. You're too honest, and Bunny doesn't have enough imagination."

"Bunny has guts, though," I pointed out.

"True," she said. "Bunny's got a lot going for her. She's who you should hang out with after I've run away."

"What do you mean, hang out with?" I asked.

"You can decide for yourself what it means. It won't be my business anymore."

I was shocked. "So you pass me on to a new girlfriend, just like that? Secondhand Jericho?"

"What makes you think I was your *old* girlfriend?"

Those three devastating comments sprang to mind, but again, I didn't get a chance to use them. Not because Alison kissed me, though. Because she burst into tears.

"Listen, forget the boy-girl stuff," I said. "It's not such a great idea to run away. How about if you talk to Fugleman? You can explain that you don't want to move to Mobile and ask him to grant you a scholarship instead."

Alison made a noise halfway between a hiccup and a giggle.

"Seriously," I said.

"I just talked with him, and he thinks it's a great idea," said Alison.

"What—a scholarship?"

"No, moving to Mobile. There's no way he'd give me a scholarship. I told him I wanted to stay at Mending Wall, but he started going on about how Mobile will be a learning experience for me, and how I only want to stay because of my teenage crush on you."

"Because of your teenage what?"

"Crush. Don't get your hopes up—he said it, not me. He gave me this speech about puberty."

"He's as bad as Douglas," I complained. "Grown-ups have dirty minds."

Alison nodded. "That's what I told him. I said I'd sooner die than have sex with you."

"Thanks a bunch!"

"I didn't mean anything personal," she told me kindly. "Anyway, he wants Mom's note. Do you know where it is? I can't find it anywhere."

"It's in my pocket," I said. "I'll go back with you and talk to him—if I explain, maybe he'll see reason."

When we went into Fugleman's study,* he was on the phone. Alison and I had to wait while he persuaded a local butcher to let us have a cow's eye to dissect in science class. I gathered that the butcher was grossed out, but Fugleman convinced him that as a result of his generosity, some Mending Wall kid might become a famous surgeon and save lives in Alcott, New Hampshire. I pretended to be watching something through the window, but actually I was paying close attention; Fugleman is a true wheeler-dealer, in an academic way, and I figured I could learn from him.

"What do you see out there?" he asked after putting down the receiver.

"Nothing much," I said. "Just admiring the view."

Fugleman loves it when you comment on the view; it gives him a chance to make this little speech which goes "It's an inspiring view. I never look out this window without feeling privileged."

I listened while he made it now. Then I set to work buttering him up.

"You did a great job with that butcher," I began. "I bet there's nothing you couldn't get people to do, you're so good at persuading them. Maybe you ought to be president."**

"What do you want, Jericho?"

---

* Fugleman refuses to call his study an office because it sounds too official. It still feels like an office, though.

** Actually, this is not such a great reason to become president. Think about it.

I reached into my pocket for Alison's mom's fern-scented pale green note, hoping that once my father read it, he'd be on our side. Only it wasn't there. All I could find was the glossy brochure I'd brought back from the future.

"Whoops!" I said.

Alison took the brochure and glanced at it absently. "This isn't it. What did you do, lose it?"

Luckily, I knew that note by heart, so I was able to recite the message for Fugleman. He seemed impressed. When I finished, he opened the file cabinet near his desk and pulled out Alison's file. I figured this was a good sign.

"Alison's mom wants to make Alison over so she looks like some ditzy fashion model," I told him. "It's spiritual rape when women try to make other women over, in case you didn't know. That's why I think you should grant Alison a scholarship so she can stay at Mending Wall."

Fugleman smiled at Alison. "Even to suggest such a thing would be gross interference on my part, given the situation."

"Are you kidding?" I said. "It's *because* of the situation that you should let her stay."

"What I'm referring to is Stanley Mifflin." Fugleman gave the file three little slaps with the palm of his hand. "It seems Alison is going to be reunited with her biological father. That's uncommon in our day and age."

"I don't understand," said Alison.

Fugleman opened the file and showed her a photocopy of her birth certificate. I looked, too. In the space marked "Name of Father," it said Stanley Mifflin.

"Didn't your mother ever tell you who your father was?" I asked.

Alison shook her head.

"Well, in any case, congratulations!" said Fugleman.

Alison turned pale and threw herself into my arms.

20 ❧ Enter Fugleman
(Honest Ending)

"Well, in any case, congratulations!" said Fugleman.
"Chill out," said Alison, and she left the room.

21 ❦ 2094

When I caught up with Alison, she was laughing.

"What's so funny?" I asked.

She held up the brochure.* "'A Jewel in New Hampshire's Glorious Past.' Where did you get this?"

"From the future," I said.

She started to laugh again and then stopped, looking down at the brochure. "You weren't kidding. You've been to 2094."

"We couldn't figure out what year exactly."

"'January 2094 Update,'" she read aloud, and, looking over her shoulder, I finally learned about observation days:

> Monday, April 12, 2094: Easter Sunday Observed
> Monday, July 5, 2094: Fourth of July Observed
> Monday, December 27, 2094: Christmas Day Observed
> Monday, January 3, 2095: New Year's Day Observed

"Crimeny!" said Alison.

---

* By the way, the brochure was full of lies. For instance that Mr. Fugleman was a rich farmer, and that kids in our time ate in the kitchen with the hired help. There were several color photos of people modeling "typical twentieth century rural styles." School-age boys, according to the brochure, often wore a cape over a blue jersey with a large red letter *S* printed on it. *S* for school.

22 ❧ Life Goes On at Mending Wall

The problem with having school in your home is that when you need a break, you're stuck. I mean, if you're a public school kid and feel like taking time off on a weekday morning, at least you have some options. For instance:

1. Admit that you have horrendous stomach cramps but say you don't want to miss the all-day field trip to the Ping-Pong Hall of Fame.

2. Act depressed when you wake up and say all you need is one day, just one day, to stay home and catch up in your work to be on top of things at school for the whole rest of the year.

I could go on, but that's enough to start with. Just remember that for the first option, it's important to insist on going to school,* and for the second it's important to have at least one gullible parent. Unfortunately, my father runs the school and is far from gullible. If I don't turn up at talkfest, he marches into my room to say, "Knock it off, Jericho. You're late for class."

Alison was a boarder, so she had the same problem. She

---

* Don't worry, someone will talk you out of it.

had been feeling like scat* ever since she got the bad news, but she wasn't running a temperature, so she had to go to class. She put up a good show, too. When things aren't going right, Alison doesn't let it all hang out—she kind of clams up and goes on automatic pilot. But I knew how she was feeling, so I was desperately searching for ideas that would cheer us up.

Toward the end of the week, the weather began to change. Thursday was a gray, blustery sort of morning. When I looked out my window, I noticed that the last of the leaves had blown off the branches overnight. It reminded me that winter wasn't far away.

"It's going to be a long, cold one," I said to the bundle in the other bed.

"A long, cold what?"

"Winter without Alison, bonehead."

BVD emerged from under the covers and ran his fingers through his hair so it stood up in a Mohawk. Then he cleared his throat. I braced myself against what was coming:

> *Alison gone*
> *blackbirds dying in the snow*
> *winter long and cold*

"You're missing a syllable in the first line," I said.

"Poetic license, asshole."

"Not with haiku," I said. "Five-seven-five, no exceptions. Plus it lacks feeling. Have you ever been in love?"

---

* Useful word. It has all the punch of standard four-letter words but no criminal record. Try it on a teacher someday.

"None of your business."

"That means no," I guessed. "If you had a girl, you'd be too busy writing about it to move in on her."

BVD belched and got out of bed, already fully dressed except for shoes.* "Soccer game today," he reminded me.

"Go on," I said. "What are the next two lines?"

I should have known better. When it comes to poetry, BVD is 99 percent humorless. So he cleared his throat again and shot two more lines at me:

> *soccer game today*
> *life goes on at Mending Wall*
> *in spite of losers*

"Speak for yourself," I said. "I might make a goal."

"I might get named poet laureate of the United States of America," said BVD.**

I wished he knew what it was like to be in love so I could ask his advice about Alison. If she really meant to run away, she was headed for disaster. Somehow, I had to make sure she stayed at Mending Wall. What if I got a judge to say her mother was irresponsible, for instance? Then I might talk Fugleman into adopting her. There had to be other options, too. The trouble with Alison was, once she went on automatic pilot, she tended to ignore the options.

"What's the big hurry?" my roommate asked, seeing me throw on my clothes and head for the door.

---

* BVD sleeps in his clothes so as to have a few extra minutes of sleep in the morning. If necessary, he changes into clean socks and underwear last thing before retiring.

** There's your remaining 1 percent.

"I need a word with Alison," I explained. "In her room, where we can have some privacy."

"Won't Bunny and Jessica be there?"

"They go running before breakfast."

True. Every weekday morning since I could remember, rain or shine, Bunny and Jessica had run three miles before breakfast. As far as I know, Jessica hasn't broken her record. Bunny has, though. That Thursday morning when I walked in, she was still there chatting with Alison.

With Alison—and Nick.

23 ❧ More Questions and Answers

I didn't know what to say. Not because he was in the girls' room—that was no big deal. But because now I knew he came from so far into the future. I mean, this kid wasn't even born yet, so to speak. I'd have to live my whole life and die before he was born, unless I grew to be a hundred.

"Yo, Jericho!" he said.

I just nodded. It was too weird to see him sitting on Alison's bed and fooling around with her Fisher-Price farm, as real as you and me. Alison, by the way, was still in her pajamas. Nothing unusual about that at Mending Wall, where kids have been known to show up for class in their pajamas. What did startle me was that she was holding a Curly Girl lipstick and painting this big red star on her chin. Her mom would have been thrilled.

"How did you like my room?" Nick asked in his pleasant talk-show voice.

"He means Maple's room," Bunny explained. "You left something there. Show him, Alison."

"That wasn't mine," I said, blushing as I remembered what she had tacked to the poster. But the thing Alison pulled out from under her pillow was not a jockstrap—it was a crumpled, pale green fern-scented envelope.

"So that's where it went!" I said. "But how did you know it was us?"

Nick flipped a Fisher-Price hen from hand to hand. "You

wrote *Perrin's drosophila* on it. Besides, people don't use scented paper in our time. We think it's gross."

"Most of us do, too," I said. But I didn't explain about Alison's mom, because I was bursting with questions about 2094. Here they are, along with Nick's answers:

1. Where was everyone in Glen Alcott the other day?
   Answer: At home. Most people in 2094 work at home, communicating with their employers by teleophones or portafax machines.* If we had hung around until their lunch break, we would have seen them all out jogging.

2. Why did the Fugleman Homestead close early that day?
   Answer: Nick's mother (the tour guide) and Nick's father (the shoe-check man) had to renew their marriage license. People can do this by portafax, but it's considered more romantic to do it in person.

3. Why did men wear makeup in 2094?
   Answer: Why not?

---

* With a teleophone, your televised image appears on a screen so you can use body language while you talk. Portafax machines are more high-tech: you get delivered along with your letter or manuscript. It's only a projection of your body, though, and can't function independently. If you've been portafaxed to Tokyo, you can't stay for sushi.

4. How on earth did people get the idea that Mending Wall had been a private home?
Answer: No one could afford to live in a big place like that, so it stood empty until rumors spread that it was haunted. As the years went by, it became a tourist attraction. Not until 2089 was it declared a historic monument. No one remembered that it had been a school.

5. There must have been records of it, though.
Answer: The concept of written records became outdated in the early twenty-first century, when computer files took over. But all the computer files in the state of New Hampshire* got zapped when a meteor fell into Lake Winnipesaukee in 2017.

6. Who is Blame?
Answer: Blame is not a person; it's a thing. A bad thing. It's socially taboo to blame anyone, including yourself. Only social renegades are into blame. In 2094, Glen Alcott prides itself on being 97 percent blame-free.

---

* Also southern Maine and eastern Vermont.

24 ❦ A Nice Place to Live, Part II

"That's weird," said Bunny. "Are there more towns like Glen Alcott?"

Nick shrugged and picked up the other Fisher-Price hen. "My dad says towns are the same all over the United States. But I couldn't say, because I've never been away from home."

"Why not?" I asked.

"What's the point of going to a place that's no different from the place you left behind? Besides, my dad has a theory that transvection is bad for your health."

"Trans-what?"

"Transvection. Don't you have that yet?"

"Tell me how it works, and I'll let you know."

Nick hesitated. "I can't tell you how it works, just what happens. You go to any participating McDonald's and use their transvector gate to a similar McDonald's anywhere else in the world. You get disintegrated when you walk through and reintegrated wherever you want to be. It's overpriced unless they're having one of their promotional sales, and the jet lag is terrible. Still, it's the only practical way to travel."

"That's teleportation," I informed him. "We don't have it yet, but I've read about it in sci-fi stories."

"Transvection," he repeated firmly. "Teleportation turned out to be a real disaster."

"What happened to airplanes?" Bunny asked.

"They turned out to be a real disaster, too."

"What did we do, run out of crude oil?"

"Of course," said Nick. "But that's not the main reason. The main reason is that there are no more airports. No interstates, either. The land was requisitioned for housing and farmland after the second civil war."

Bunny's eyes grew large. "The *second* civil war? What was that about?"

"Overpopulation," said Nick.

There was a long silence, during which Bunny and I moved to the window. We were thinking about the same thing: those future condominiums in Floyd's field. What we actually saw was Jessica, panting up the driveway in her running shorts. She looked sulky.

I nudged Bunny. "Hey, what do you know—for once, Jessica has an expression on her face!"

"A strange boy walked into the room while she and I were on our way out," Bunny explained, grinning at Nick. "She was shocked. So maybe we should meet somewhere else next time."

Nick nodded. "Can you come visit me this afternoon?"

"We've got a soccer game."

"What about tomorrow, then—or does everyone go home for the weekend?"

"Bunny does," I said. "Alison and I stay here."

Bunny's nose twitched. "If there's anything going on, I can stay late. I live just a couple of miles away."

We looked expectantly at Nick.

"How about a picnic?" he suggested.

"Terminal!" said Alison.

"Potluck," Nick added hastily.

"What's terminal potluck?" asked Bunny.

"*Terminal* means cool," I explained. "*Potluck* just means bring your own food and swap around."

Nick tossed the Fisher-Price hens into the air and began to juggle them.

"Careful!" cried Alison. "Those are collector's items. They don't make them the same these days."

"They don't make them at all in my time," said Nick. "They were outlawed about seven years ago."

A shiver ran through me. Then I reminded myself that seven years ago for him meant 2087. "They're going to outlaw all toys, or just Fisher-Price?"

"Hens," he said. "The USDA outlawed hens because they're unsanitary. There's a thousand-dollar fine for anyone caught trying to hatch a hen egg."

"But where do you get the eggs in the first place if you can't have hens?" asked Alison.

"Transpropagation,* like most other food." A gleam came into Nick's eye as he added, "Is it legal for you to buy hen meat without a prescription? Can you get me some?"

"Sure," I said. "It's called chicken, though. We'll bring it sometime tomorrow afternoon."

"*Sometime* won't do," he warned me. "The tours start on

---

* I found out later what this meant, and I'm not going to tell you. It may not be unsanitary, but it sure is gross.

the hour, and my mother takes them straight to the kitchen. Try to come between half past the hour and about five of."

The breakfast bell rang. Nick stood up to go, but Alison said, "You'd better wait. The kitchen is where we all eat, and after that there's talkfest. Want to come to talkfest? They allow visitors."

Nick shook his head. "Too risky. I'll wait here, and one of you can tell me when it's safe to leave."

"I'll do that," Alison promised, pulling on her navy sweatshirt as she headed for the door. "By the way, what was that about your parents renewing their marriage license?"

"Their old one expired," Nick explained. "You have to renew them every two years. Plus you have to take the test again if you have a bad record or you want to have kids."

Alison stopped short. Bunny and I were following right behind, so we bumped into her.

"Do you mind?" Bunny said crossly.

"Yes," said Alison. "Let me get this straight—in Glen Alcott, couples have to pass a test in order to get married? And another one if they want to have kids?"

Nick nodded.

"Is it a hard test?"

He nodded again. "A lot of couples flunk."

"Move!" Bunny said, prodding Alison impatiently. "And in case you haven't noticed, there's a red star on your chin."

Alison ignored her. "A lot of couples flunk?" she repeated. Suddenly she got all flushed and starry-eyed. "What a nice place to live!"

Bunny quit acting impatient. Instead, her face lit up as if

she had been struck by a brilliant idea. I was too dumb to ask her about it or believe me, I would have nipped it in the bud.*

---

* Nick had to wait two hours until the coast was clear, but he wasn't bored. He claimed to have spent the time browsing through some historical novels he found in Jessica's bookshelf. It turned out that he meant *Sweet Valley High.*

25 ❦ Mending Wall vs. Alcott Middle School

If you've been waiting impatiently for this chapter, forget it. I'm not about to give a blow-by-blow account of the sporting event of the season. However, I admit there has been more talk than action so far. It's time for a little action, and the best place to find it is out on the Mending Wall soccer field—which slopes, remember? And remember the dead elm in front of the uphill goal? And our goats? Need I say more?

Okay, now I'm going to get you into the mood. Imagine a gray, blustery sort of afternoon. This is good; at least the sun isn't in anybody's eyes. The field is in pretty good shape, too. We don't have to mow it because the goats keep the grass down. We don't have to fertilize it either. Guess why. Our only problem is how to keep the goats from joining in the game.

Got the picture? Now add the home team. As you must know, there are eleven men* on a soccer team. Add our two juniors to our six seniors, and what have you got? A defective team. Or, according to Douglas, quality as opposed to quantity. When Alcott Middle School has a game with us, they have to lend us three players. So imagine eight kids ranging from age eight to age fourteen, and from four-foot-

---

* I just got an elbow jab from Bunny, who has been reading over my shoulder. Okay, *players.* Eleven players.

one to five-eleven. Paint them every color of the rainbow (*uniform* is a dirty word at Mending Wall—we're encouraged to be rugged individualists, and we dress that way).

The rest is easy. All you have left to imagine is twenty-two kids from Alcott Middle School. Yes, I said twenty-two: they keep a full spare team sitting on the bench. Imagine them all the same height, give or take an inch or two. All the same age, give or take a month or two. Dress them in red T-shirts with big black letters that say ALCOTT RAMS. What have you got? Rams and goats. Or winners and losers, if you want to be crude about it. You choose.

Don't get me wrong, though. We put up a good fight. Some of our best assets are unconventional, but since the odds are against us, we're not ashamed to use them. For instance, when you've got a kid on your team who barely comes up to the opponent's belly button, you can't expect her to run faster or kick harder. So how do you use her? For tripping people up. No, she doesn't stick her leg out when they run by; that would bring us penalties. She just stands there, well below eye level. It works every time.

On Thursday afternoon, Douglas and Fugleman had taken the pickup to collect a shipment of school supplies— a relief to most of us. Douglas is a good coach, but if he feels that you've let the team down, he looks at you with sad, sad eyes. As for Fugleman, he's such a believer in rugged individualism that if we break a rule for reasons he approves of, he won't let the referee blow the whistle on us. This makes him unpopular with visiting teams.

So we're left with Cathleen. Cathleen is a good coach, too. She's very supportive and usually sends someone down to the Grand Union for a bag of oranges to pass out during halftime. Her only problem is when she gets emotionally involved and joins the game. She makes a lot of goals for us, but none of them count.

"Okay," you're saying. "I've got the picture, but where's the action?"

I'll give you the last few minutes of the last quarter. Don't complain—that will be all you can take, believe me. Ready?

26 ❦ Action

Jessica, Maple, Zoë, and two borrowed Rams make up the forward line. Jason is center halfback, with another Ram to either side. BVD and Bunny play defense, and I'm goalie. Where's Alison? She never showed up. I don't have time to look for her because as usual, the ball is near our goal. It's our turn for the uphill side, meaning it's harder for the other team to run or kick, and the dead elm is in their way. They've scored four goals so far. We've scored three, but they were all made by Cathleen, so they don't count. In other words, even with some of their players on our side, the Rams are winning.

Cathleen is in a good mood. She thinks it has been a great game. She couldn't care less that those goals didn't count. Once or twice she gets the teams mixed up and starts cheering for the other side, and when the referee yells at her,* she blows him a kiss.

One of the forwards from the Alcott team has the ball now and is nudging it gently toward our goal. Jason and Jessica trip each other up trying to get it away from him. Zoë is puffing along about a foot behind him, steadily losing ground.

Cathleen yells, "Way to go, Zoë!"

Zoë stops to wave.

---

* For dashing into the field to wipe Maple's runny nose.

A few yards away from me, Bunny groans. She leaps nervously from one side of the goal box to the other, unable to make up her mind where she'll be needed next. Don't laugh—she's doing the best she can, considering that BVD is lounging against the dead elm, quoting Robert Frost.

BVD says, "'Oh, just another kind of outdoor game, / One on a side.'"*

I say, "Holy Moses, BVD!"

The Alcott forward draws nearer. Confident. Taking his own sweet time.

Cathleen yells, "Way to go, Maple!"

I can't see Maple. I worry. What's she up to? The Alcott forward swerves, then falls flat on his face. Sorry, make that flat on Maple. Maple grabs the ball.

The whistle blows. "Dangerous play!" the ref shouts disgustedly. He thinks again and adds, "Hand ball!"

Maple plays dead.

Cathleen rushes in, picks her up, and carries her off the field. No one worries; we all know Maple is faking.

Alison turns up all of a sudden, no apologies. Cathleen sends her in to take Maple's place as center forward. There's still a red star on Alison's chin, and she isn't wearing cleats—just socks. Luckily, the ref doesn't notice.

The game resumes. An Alcott halfback gets to make an indirect kick. The ball heads for the elm. BVD wakes up, intercepts the ball, and gives it another kick—straight into our goal.

They won.

---

* Another line from the poem "Mending Wall." Needless to say, it doesn't refer to soccer.

27 ❦ Lois and Fred and the Fisher-Price Hen

You're not going to believe this. I didn't myself. But for what it's worth, here's a conversation that took place right after the game. Cast of characters: Alison, Jessica, Jericho.

Jericho: (*Gloomily*) They won.

Alison: (*Casually*) So what's new?

Jessica: (*Primly*) You know what, Alison? If you had a little team spirit, we might win a game once in a while. Where the heck were you, anyway?

Alison: On the john.

Jessica: Yeah, sure!

Jericho: Chill out, Jessica. So she was taking a crap— what makes it your business?

Jessica: I bet she was with that guy who barged into our room this morning.

Jericho: You're so jealous, I bet you pee green! (*Exit Jessica, in a huff.*)

Alison: Thanks, Jericho. She was right, though.

Jericho: What do you mean?

Alison: I *was* with Nick.

Jericho: You mean he came back?

Alison: I went to his time. I couldn't find him, though, so I came straight home.

Jericho: What did you go for in the first place?

Alison: He took my Fisher-Price hen.

Jericho: That's a reason?

Alison: (*Silence, served with a reproachful look*)

Jericho: You're lucky you didn't get caught.

Alison: I did. Fred and Lois caught me.

Jericho: Who in the name of blame are Fred and Lois?

Alison: Nick's parents. They didn't see me arrive, but they tracked me down later because my cleats left mud all over the floor.

Jericho: My God! What did they do?

Alison: They confiscated my cleats, but apart from that, they were so-o-o nice to me! Oh, Jericho—they're terminal!

Jericho: You mean the man with the makeup and that lady who was all dressed up like an organ grinder's monkey? You've got to be kidding—they're the pits!

Alison: They liked me. They even asked me to come back. Lois says she could use an assistant with the tour groups, so I said I'd help out after school.

Jericho: Fun, fun, fun.

28 ❧ Grand Union; Not So Grand Reunion

It isn't easy to raid the fridge at Mending Wall. Not that it's off limits or anything—ever since the Sugar War, Fugleman has kept it crammed with healthful snacks for us to eat anytime we want. The problem is that they aren't the sort of snacks you feel like raiding, not to mention bringing to a picnic.

"There's plenty of my homemade yogurt left," Alison said on Friday afternoon, as we stood looking at the grim assortment of low-fat cheeses and raw vegetables.

Bunny and I kept a polite silence.

"We could use it for dip and eat it with celery sticks."

"Okay," I agreed, "but Nick is going to get a weird idea of what food is like in our time. Besides, we said we'd bring chicken."

"Anybody got cash?" Bunny asked. "I could take the bike* down to the Grand Union. They sell cooked chicken in the deli, and I could buy some Ding-Dongs."

Alison produced a ten-dollar bill. "Mom gave it to me for when I take the plane," she said.

"Then keep it," said Bunny. "You might want to buy a magazine or something."

* That's right, *the* bike. Don't ask me why there's only one at Mending Wall when every kid has his own cross-country skis. It's an old balloon-tire contraption, and we share it.

"I'm not taking any plane," said Alison.

This was Friday during study hall. Alison had to finish a paper on genetic variability,* and I'd promised Cathleen to teach Creative Repairs to the juniors so she could straighten out the Mending Wall accounts. So it was Bunny who biked into town and came back with the following items in a Grand Union plastic shopping bag:

> A pound of barbecued chicken wings
> A bag of restaurant-style nacho chips
> Four organic tangerines
> A six-pack of beer
> Twenty-nine cents

"They were out of Ding-Dongs," she announced.

"Twenty-nine cents?" Alison protested. "That's all the change you got, was twenty-nine cents?"

Bunny was indignant. "You should be thanking me! The beer was on sale."

"I don't even *like* beer," said Alison.

Bunny doesn't look one day over her age, which is thirteen. It was hard to believe that anyone had sold beer to her in the first place. Not even some weird brand that happened to be on sale. So I picked up a can and looked at it more carefully. It turned out to be nonalcoholic.

"You did okay," I reassured her. "Nick said he'd bring stuff, too, and we can swap around."

Alison gave Bunny a frosty look, but she stopped com-

---

* She tested the whole school for two hereditary traits: mid-digital hair and hitchhiker's thumb. I had both.

plaining. I gave Bunny a different kind of look; her eyes were shining, and her face was pink. Her black velvet headband had slipped some, so this little damp curl had escaped and was stuck to her left cheek. It struck me that she'd be a good person to take a bike ride with someday.

"How did your class go?" she asked me.

"Not bad," I said. "Only problem was I tested Zoë on the kitchen shut-off valves, and something has been banging away back in the crawl space ever since. Do you suppose some air got locked into the system?"

"Either that or Zoë," said Bunny.

It turned out she was right. When Maple and I left the crawl space, Zoë stayed behind. Why? Because she found the sugar stash and stayed until she had eaten every last kernel of candy corn.* Then she got scared and started banging on the pipes. Why didn't she just yell? Because she was afraid she'd throw up if she opened her mouth.

"What you need is fresh air," said Bunny.

Zoë said what she needed was her mother. It was already half past three, but we couldn't leave until the kitchen was clear, so Bunny led her off to find Cathleen. This took a while; Cathleen always hides when she does the Mending Wall accounts. They demand a lot of juggling, which she can't do if she's constantly interrupted. Bunny finally tracked her down in the furnace room, but it was one minute to four by the time we left for the future.

Nick was in the kitchen of the Fugleman Homestead, impatiently waiting for us. "What took you so long?"

---

* You guessed it—Cathleen doesn't let nonessential carbohydrates into her home either, so Zoë had to fill up while she had the chance.

I started to explain about Zoë, but he interrupted me. "Quick, take off your shoes! My parents have been complaining about black-and-white boots with spikes. They confiscated a pair just yesterday."

"They're mine," said Alison. "Can I have them back?"

"Why would a girl want to wear boots with spikes?"

"Soccer players, *including females,* wear cleats—not spikes—to insure traction," Bunny informed him with a dangerous note in her voice.

Nick tapped his forehead in the same odd way that he had done the first time I met him, after he spilled Alison's fruit flies. "No blame," he said gently.

"No blame?" Bunny's eyes flashed. "You're damn right there's no blame! I kind of assumed these were enlightened times. What happened to women's lib?"

Alison said, "Chill out, Bunny! Nick isn't blaming women's lib. All he's trying to say is that he didn't mean to offend you."

"That's right," Nick agreed. "What's women's lib?"

Things were going from bad to worse. I tried to present women's lib in terms that would appease Bunny, but I kept saying the wrong thing. Want to know what made her calm down in the end? It was when Nick said they didn't have women's lib in 2094—what they had instead was hemancipation.

"What's hemancipation?" Bunny asked.

"It's a movement promoting the rights of he-men," Nick explained. "Just because certain males are muscle-bound and undersensitized doesn't mean they should be the objects of public derision and prejudice."

That took Bunny's breath away, so she didn't answer

when Nick inquired politely why the spikes on our soccer shoes didn't mess up our courts. I asked him what he meant by courts, and by the time he had explained how soccer was played in 2094,* the atmosphere had cleared. Only for a moment, though. Only until we were safely out of the Homestead and I handed him our shopping bag.

Nick quit talking instantly. An expression of embarrassed horror spread over his face. "What's that?"

"Food. For the picnic."

He cast an apprehensive look over his shoulder before whispering, "I mean, what's that thing you put the food *in?*"

I guessed what the problem was. "As a matter of fact, plastic bags are frowned on in our time, too. Fugleman won't let us use them. When we shop, we're supposed to bring our own reusable canvas bags. Bunny should have known better."

"I beg your pardon!" Bunny snapped, glaring at me. "Speak for yourself, Jerko."

Nick gestured anxiously. "You don't understand. The plastic isn't the problem—it's the writing. Hide it!"

I took out the chicken, the nacho chips, the fruit, and the beer. Then I turned the bag inside out and put everything back in again. It was the flimsy kind, so you could still read the letters, only now they spelled NOINU DNARG.

"Is that better?" I asked. When Nick looked doubtful, I added, "Maybe you should explain."

---

* On courts with a synthetic, spongy surface. The players wear light-weight slippers with resin-treated soles. The soccer balls in Nick's time are petropneumatic, which I can't explain without getting scientific. The main thing is, they're painless to kick.

So Nick explained. The Grand Union was (or rather, will be) a fun-loving religious sect that got banned by the government in 2069 for overstepping the limits of decency even by the standards of what Bunny calls enlightened times. By 2094, it was socially taboo to mention it.

Bunny giggled. "But the Grand Union is a supermarket!"

"Could you lower your voice?" Nick looked over his shoulder again. "They deal in hen meat, don't they? Someone might hear and report you to the authorities."

"What authorities?"* asked Bunny. "You're chicken!"

Nick's face flushed with anger. "No one calls me unsanitary and gets away with it!"

I could see that if I didn't put my patience, tact, and reckless loyalty to work, the picnic would end before Nick had a chance to sample hen meat.

"Hey, guys," I said soothingly. "No blame!"

---

* It turned out that by *authorities*, Nick meant the USSB, standing for United States School Board. Apparently, if you were found guilty of nonconformity of any sort, you were banned from public appearances on nationwide TV. Big deal.

29 ❧ Anachronisms

Nick wanted to picnic on the campus, but we overruled him. What's the point of traveling a hundred years into the future just to picnic in your own backyard?

"Why don't you take us to see your school?" I asked.

"Or a soccer game," Bunny suggested.

Nick wasn't keen on either idea, but he finally agreed to both since there was a match that afternoon at Glen Alcott Junior High. First he made us change clothes, though. We went to his room, where he found a bunch of tunics and tights. Luckily, we were all about the same size.

Bunny thought it was a great idea that men and women dressed the same. Alison thought it was a pain in the neck. As I said before, she went everywhere in the same old jeans and navy sweatshirt.

"And I thought you did, too," she said to Nick.

"Just around the house," he explained. "If I wore a costume in town, people would stare."

"Costume?"

"Costume," he repeated. "I got the pants and top out of the costume display. 'Late Twentieth Century, Typical Young Male Attire'—females of the same age wore skirts."

Bunny opened her mouth to protest, but he forestalled her. "I know, I know. Remember, a lot of records were destroyed. And it's lucky I was in costume when I came to your time. Dressed like this, I would have caused a riot."

"Not at Mending Wall," said Alison.

Bunny looked at him curiously. "Why *did* you come?"

There was a long silence, during which Nick inspected us for anachronisms.* We didn't interrupt it; Bunny's question had obviously raised a touchy issue for him.

"I'm spoiled," he said at last.

This was so unexpected that I laughed.

"Seriously!" Nick insisted. "These are crowded times. The country is overpopulated—even rural areas like this."

I glanced out the window—Maple's old window, with its view over the woods and hills. Condos and hills, in Nick's time. "Rural?"

"Rural," he said. "Four-story buildings only. It's a rural zoning regulation."

Bunny raised her eyebrows. "What are the urban areas like, then?"

"Crowded," said Nick. "The point is, even in rural areas, there are laws about housing. So many rooms per family and all that. When I say I'm spoiled, I mean because I live in this house. My parents are caretakers, so they get to use some of the rooms. They wouldn't be legally eligible if it weren't for my sister."

"You have a sister? How come you never mentioned her before?"

Nick looked uncomfortable, and didn't answer for a while. "You wouldn't report us," he said finally. It was a statement, not a question.

---

* An anachronism is something historically out of place. All Nick removed was Bunny's black velvet headband, which was a vast improvement.

We shook our heads.

"When my parents applied for the job, they pretended they had two kids. The job description specified a four-member family, minimum. My mother faked a birth certificate. She's artistic — she designed the brochure for the Homestead, in case you wondered."

"Nice," I said politely, although it wasn't.

"Well, so they pretended I had this sister, Rachel, and no one ever asked to see her as proof or anything. So if it weren't for Rachel, we'd be living in one of those condos, packed in like sardines."

"That would be awful," Bunny said.

"It would," Nick agreed. "I like space. That's why I dress up in the costumes and pretend I'm living back in pioneer times, when there was a lot of it. And the other day, I measured myself against those markings on the wall to see which kid in your family I could—well, pretend to be. And all of a sudden, I was there."

"School, not family," I reminded him. I didn't take him up on "pioneer times," though. Knowing from experience how easy it is to get confused in American history.

"How does it work?" Bunny asked. "The passage from our time to yours, I mean."

Nick shrugged. "How should I know? All I can think is that it's some kind of natural transvector gate."

"But how come no one else has used it?"

"There must be some special condition," he said thoughtfully. "Something we do that no one else ever did."

Bunny shivered. "I sure hope I don't forget to do whatever it is and get stuck on the wrong side."

"Which one is the wrong side?" asked Alison.

Bunny flashed her a meaningful smile. "That depends which side you want to be on. Get it?"

Alison didn't answer. Why not? Because she *didn't* get it. Believe it or not, I didn't either.

30 ❦ Potluck

Maybe *you* got it. Bunny's brilliant idea, I mean, that I first mentioned at the end of chapter 24. Here it is: she knew Alison would rather disappear off the face of the earth than get remade into a Curly Girl. That being so, why shouldn't Alison disappear to a place where we could visit her? Or better yet (you guessed it!) to the same place—but in a different time.

When I say *brilliant,* naturally I mean from Bunny's point of view. Personally, I thought it stank. Plus I was kind of stunned when Bunny told me, which was right smack in the middle of the twenty-first century soccer match. That's why I'm unable to give you a blow-by-blow account of the action. Maybe you don't *want* a blow-by-blow account. Maybe you're like me and Alison, and think soccer is more fun to play than to watch. All you really need to know is that the home team was playing Passumpsic, a Vermont village that didn't even have its own grade school in my time but had grown into a teeming metropolis. When we arrived, there was already quite a crowd. Nick explained that this was because the Passumpsic team had been bused in. Soccer matches were common enough, but you hardly ever saw a bus.*

---

* This one was solar powered, which impressed Bunny, even after Nick told her that its top speed was 38 mph.

We sat way back behind the crowd, to avoid people noticing our nonconformity and reporting us to the USSB. As a result, we were a long way from the action. This didn't bother me. It didn't bother Nick either, who was too busy eating chicken wings. Bunny was the only one who paid attention. After dropping her bombshell of a so-called brilliant idea, she gave the match her full attention. She claims it was boring. She claims that when the players are kicking a petropneumatic ball around a synthetic surface with resin-treated slippers, you don't get to see a whole lot of dangerous plays or other good stuff like that. Passumpsic won, but it was hard to care.

The school was boring, too, in case you're wondering. Nick took us around during halftime, and the only big difference from our own public schools, as far as I could see, was that the surface of each desk was a computer. Plus there was an enormous screen at the front of every classroom where blackboards used to be.

"How long is your average school day?" I asked Nick.

He said, "Nine to three, unless you stay late for sports or band practice."

See what I mean? Boring!

Alison said I was wrong to be disappointed, that school was school wherever you went. A pretty weird statement from a kid in her fifth year at Mending Wall. But then, Alison fell for Glen Alcott right from the start. It was no use pointing out the urbanization, overpopulation, transpropagation, and boring soccer games. She still thought it was a nice place to live. In fact, the only thing she complained about all afternoon was the dessert.

"What the heck is this?" she mumbled into her first bite

of something brown and gooey that Nick had passed around.

"Ding-Dongs," he said. "Don't you have them yet in your time?"

Leaning carefully over the space between the bleachers, Alison spat. "We have them, but they're not the same. Ours are bigger and better, and they don't taste of fish."

"I'm afraid the fishy taste is one of the side effects of transpropagation," Nick said pleasantly.

Alison smiled at him. "No blame. But you'll understand when you taste the old-fashioned kind. Let's have another picnic on Sunday. Your time or ours?"

"Yours," said Nick. "When should I show up?"

"Somewhere around noon?" I suggested.

But Bunny shook her head. "Not Sunday, Jericho. Sunday is Fall Frolics, remember?"*

"So what?" I asked. "That makes it even better. More weirdos come to Mending Wall for Fall Frolics than any other day of the year, so Nick won't stick out like a sore thumb."

I was afraid that sounded rude, but Nick didn't seem to mind. "Sunday at noon, then," he agreed.

He looked cautiously around us before adding in a low voice, "And if you happen to go by the you-know-where, could you buy more hen meat?"

---

* Actually, I had forgotten Fall Frolics. You're going to hear about it in detail later on, so all I'll say is that it's an event designed by Fugleman to impress people with our youthful intelligence, good health, and high spirits.

31 ❦ Three Nice Things about Glen Alcott

Cathleen is always telling us, "If you don't have anything nice to say, don't say anything at all."

This drives Fugleman crazy. According to him, a school that encourages kids to shut up except for when they say nice things is a school that nurtures mediocrity. But the point is that so far, I haven't said a single nice thing about Glen Alcott. Sorry about that, Cathleen! I don't happen to think Glen Alcott is a nice place to live, but I hereby promise to write down three nice things about it before I go on with my story.

1. Nick swore up and down that no one got sick anymore. He claimed this was because no one smoked or ate or did any of the things that could make you sick back in our time. Not ever, even to celebrate. Bunny says I should include this in my list. Personally, I'm not so sure.

2. The soft drinks were terminal. Nick bought us some out of a vending machine.

3. Toxic Shock was terminal, too. Nick played a few of their hits for us on a new audio system called Omnisonics that was set up in his room. We

wanted to stay and hear more but Bunny said she'd be in deep scat with her parents if she didn't get back before dark.

32 ❦ Moonstruck in 1994

Unfortunately, night had fallen by the time we got back to Mending Wall. We had missed supper, for sure, so Bunny wasn't the only one in deep scat.

"You'd better leave for home before Fugleman catches you," I warned her. "No use getting in trouble both places."

"Walk me home," said Bunny.

"Are you kidding? Then I'd be in double trouble here."

"You'll be in triple trouble if I get murdered on the way."

"What are you, paranoid?"

"I just happen to be scared of the dark," said Bunny. "It's a common phobia. Want to make something of it?"

"What do you think is out there?"

"Cows," she said.

"Take the bike," I suggested. "You can outbike a cow,* can't you?"

"No lights."

"So what? There's a full moon."

Bunny's nose twitched.

Alison said, "Crimeny, Jericho! If you don't want to walk her home, I will."

This was insulting, so I told Alison to go to bed, and I walked Bunny home. But notice how no one asked how I

---

* I said this to reassure her, but I wouldn't advise you to race a cow. Not on its own territory, anyway. You'd lose.

felt about walking myself back again. Alone, through all those cows. Not that I minded—I *like* the dark. You can smell things better. Cows, for instance. Plus it was a balmy night. Clouds kept blowing across the moon. We took a shortcut across Floyd's fields, and Bunny held my hand.

"Your phobia is your own personal business," I said, "but has it ever occurred to you that it keeps you from enjoying more than 50 percent of the day for more than 50 percent of the year?"*

"I'm not holding your hand because I'm scared of the dark," said Bunny. "I'm holding your hand because I happen to feel like holding your hand. Okay?"

"Okay," I said. And I had no objection, even though I was a little steamed at her for thinking it was a brilliant idea to move Alison to another century.

It's over a mile to Bunny's house, taking the shortcut. We didn't hurry because even by moonlight, a cow can look like a rock. You walk past unsuspecting, and suddenly it heaves to its feet and trots away. Every time this happened, Bunny screamed. Between screams we had a good conversation, though. Mainly about whether we'd go bonkers if we had to live in Glen Alcott. We agreed that we would, unless we had been born there. Maybe even then.

After a while we came to where the field slopes down to the road again. It's so steep that Floyd can't mow there without tipping over his tractor. Bunny and I had just slithered down it when we heard voices. Naturally we froze.

---

* This only applies to people who are scared of the dark and live a long way from the equator, in case you wondered.

"Biodegradable" was the first word we could hear clearly. A woman said it.

I whispered, "That's Cathleen."

"Shut up!" whispered Bunny.

Footsteps came closer, sending pebbles skittering along the dirt road. There was also a weird scrunching kind of noise. We couldn't see anyone yet.

"Granted, but you're not taking account of pre-consumer manufacturing techniques," a man's voice said.

That's really what he said—I swear! A man and woman are out walking on a balmy moonlit night, and they're discussing pre-consumer manufacturing techniques?

"That's Douglas," Bunny whispered.

I didn't tell her to shut up. What I did was put my arm around her waist.

Cathleen's face came into sight, round and pale in the moonlight, like the moon. "Statistics prove that they've been minimized. Anyway, what's the alternative?"

"Enlightenment," Douglas stated. "Education leads to cooperation." Now I could see him, too.

Cathleen said, "And meanwhile, we continue to squander Earth's resources? How can you be so jejune?"

Bunny nudged me. "What the heck is 'jejune'?"

"What the heck are they pushing?" I whispered.

It was a shopping cart.

I'm sorry. I couldn't help it. I burst out laughing, and a split second later, so did Bunny.

Douglas's voice cracked like a whip into the darkness. "Who's there?"

One of them switched on a flashlight. That was Douglas,

too, I'd guess, because Cathleen was pushing the cart. We tried to scrunch down in the unmown grass, but there wasn't enough of it to hide in, and the flashlight was coming closer.

"Run!" said Bunny.

We slithered up the slope again. Then we ran. Not immediately, though. First we mooned them.

33 ❦ Fugleman's Fury

Boy, was my father mad!

"What were you doing out there?" he demanded after hanging up the phone on Cathleen's outraged complaints.

"Walking Bunny home," I said. "What were *they* doing out there?"

Can you believe this? It seems they were picking the last of the season's apples. By moonlight. With a Grand Union shopping cart that was a long, long way from home.

"Whose cart?" I asked. "Whose apples?"

He didn't answer that one. "With your convoluted prepubescent mind, I have no doubt that you attributed more prurient motives to their nocturnal expedition."*

"After last night, I'm giving up on Cathleen and Douglas," I said. "They'll never get around to trying anything like that. They talk too much."

The good news is that he didn't say a word about mooning. Why not? Because that's not what shocked him. What shocked him was that Bunny and I laughed at Cathleen and Douglas, thereby assaulting their spiritual privacy.

---

* Do you realize there are six fancy words in that sentence? I'll give you a break and translate. Fugleman meant that with my dirty mind, I probably thought Cathleen and Douglas were out there for something to do with sex. He was right.

"Would that be like spiritual rape?" I asked.

"Worse," said Fugleman.

See what I mean about Mending Wall?

34 ❦ Alison's Advice

"You did *what?*"

Alison had just come out of the shower and was headed for bed. She stood there wrapped in a towel, staring at me while the drips from her hair formed puddles.

"We mooned Cathleen and Douglas," I repeated.

"You mean you pulled down your pants and—and exposed your butts?"

"That's how you do it," I agreed.

"What for?"

"Why not?"

"Please be serious, Jericho."

"We did it because it was a wild, windy night, and the moon was full, and Cathleen and Douglas were squandering Earth's resources."

Alison narrowed her eyes at me. "How about you and Bunny? Were *you* squandering Earth's resources?"

"None of your business," I said.

"Want my advice?" she asked.

"Not particularly," I said.

"Grow up," said Alison.

35 ❧ The Wing of Friendship Moults?

I realize that I told you all this good stuff about Alison back at the beginning, and maybe you think she isn't living up to her reputation. Well, what did you expect? In just one week she was moving to Mobile, Alabama, leaving her best friend behind.

Yes, *friend.* Just because she was mad at me for baring my butt with another girl and I was mad at her for minding, it didn't mean that we weren't still friends.

Let's take a trip to the past for a change. All the way back to February 14, 1992. I happen to know that Jessica sent BVD a homemade valentine claiming that she was his, body and soul. Maple, who wasn't even a junior yet, sent a valentine to Jason. I won't repeat what it said because I'm trying to keep this story clean. Besides, I'm pretty sure Maple didn't know what she was writing.*

What's the point? The point is that when the whole rest of Mending Wall was sticky with passion and candy hearts, Alison and I had a *Bartlett's* battle.** We must have sent about twenty homemade cards back and forth, trying to see who could find the best quote about friendship. Alison's fa-

---

* I found out later that it was copied word for word from page 19, lines 3 and 4 of the good old Sex Ed textbook.

** *Bartlett's* is a dictionary of quotations. Don't worry—I'm not going to send you to look anything up in it.

vorite was by a poet named Byron who wrote that "Friendship is Love without his wings!"

I didn't go for that one—it made friendship sound differently advantaged in a wimpy way. So I found a quote by Charles Dickens where "the wing of friendship never moults a feather."

Alison objected, naturally. She said she preferred friendship to have no wings at all than to make like a chicken. And ever since then, after we've had a difference of opinion, she's sent me a feather in the mail. Anonymously: no comment necessary.

Who won the *Bartlett's* battle? What a dumb question! When you're friends like me and Alison, it's always a draw.

36 🌱 Fall Frolics

I'm painting another picture for you. Ready?

It's the second Sunday in November. Summer is shrouded in the mists of time, and fall foliage has reached its glorious, gaudy peak in scenic New Hampshire.* Are you gagging yet? Me, too. I copied that sentence out of a state tourism brochure. Actually, it doesn't apply; by November thirteen, the trees are bare. So are the roads. No more tourist buses with tinted windows cruising along Route Two.

Does life go on at Mending Wall? Not this time. Not as usual, anyway. So bring out the balloons. Paint the campus with Thanksgiving colors: mostly brown. If you want to get fancy, make it a scratch-'n'-sniff affair: wood smoke and apple cider. Also the ever-present aroma of our goats. Gagging again? Let's proceed to sound.

Put in some voices: Fugleman's bossy bark and Cathleen's coo. Juniors squealing. Seniors playing it cool in case someone suspects they're having fun. Parents making parent noises. It's Fall Frolics day—whoopee!

See all those pieces of pink paper lying around the grounds? Those are programs. People tend to drop them. If you pick one up and look at it, this is what you'll read:

---

* Where, according to our license plates, you can live free or die. It's true, it's true! Some people even do both.

FALL FROLICS 1994
*O hushed October morning mild!**

12:00 Reading: "Mending Wall," by Robert Frost

12:05 Convocation

12:25 "Reverie" for solo flute
Composer: Jessica Fusco, Senior
Flautist: Jessica Fusco, Senior

12:30 Hymn and Processional:
"Mending Wall, We Cherish Thee"
(All verses, words on the back of your program)

12:35 Barbecue Dinner
(Dessert coupons for sale in mud room)

1:00 Silent Auction

1:30 Three-legged Race

1:45 Egg Toss

2:00 Student-Faculty Tug-of-War

2:30 Nature Walk (optional)

* This is the first line from a Robert Frost poem called "October." It's kind of inappropriate, considering that Fall Frolics is noisy, takes place in November, and doesn't really get going until noon.

One thing I wasn't counting on when I told Nick to come at noon: the convocation takes place in the kitchen. I should have thought of this, of course. It wasn't all that warm outside. Even if it had been, no one wanted to move dozens of chairs out only to bring them back in again. The problem was that when Nick popped out of the wall, he'd find himself in a crowd of at least sixty people.*

"Let's rearrange the chairs," Bunny suggested. "Line them up so everyone has their backs to the height chart."

"That's not such a bad idea," I said. "There are just two disadvantages: Fugleman and Jessica."

"Fugleman won't notice," said Bunny. "When he starts shooting his mouth off, the whole audience could strip naked and he wouldn't notice."

This was not only an exaggeration, it was downright insulting. I didn't take her up on it, though.

"Jessica would notice," I pointed out. She'll recognize Nick, and she'll have a fit. I wonder what effect that would have on 'Reverie'?"

"'Reverie' already sounds like someone having a fit," said Alison.

I was in a tolerant mood that morning, so I didn't take Alison up on her remark either, although it was inaccurate.**

"We can't afford to take risks," I told the girls. "We'll

---

* Mainly locals who want to check out the weirdos at Mending Wall. Parents come, too, but not Alison's mom. She's never been—not even once.

** "Reverie" doesn't sound in the least like someone having a fit. It sounds like tepid bathwater going very slowly down a clogged-up drain.

move the chairs, and then the three of us should reserve seats in the back row under the height chart. Except we won't sit in them—we'll stand so we make a screen for Nick when he arrives."

Neither of them bothered to congratulate me on this plan, so I'll take the opportunity to say that not only was it brilliant, it also worked. Nick arrived suddenly in the middle of Fugleman's line about *campus* meaning field in Latin. No one saw him do it. The only hitch was that I happened to be leaning against the wall at the time, so he accidentally knocked me forward over the seat in front of me. Douglas's mom was sitting in it. She thinks the inmates of Mending Wall School are all loonies, so she just gave me a weary glance. So did Fugleman, but he went on shooting his mouth off, as Bunny puts it.

"Yo, Jericho!" said Nick. "What's up? Why is that guy shooting his mouth off?"

I gave Nick an unamused glance and handed him my program. "Shhh! He's my father. He's delivering the convocation speech."

"In person?"*

Fugleman said, "You in the back row—would it be asking too much to show some consideration for the speaker?"

He noticed Nick then, but assumed he was a visitor. From our own time, not the future. Which is what we told anyone who asked that day, starting with Jessica, who had been sitting down the row from us.

---

* Nick explained later that school principals speak from the office in 2094. The kids all stay in their classrooms and watch on those big screens we'd noticed the other day.

"Isn't it about time you introduced your friend?" she asked Alison as she inched by us on her way up to play "Reverie." "The other morning, you forgot."

It was a challenge, and Alison accepted it. "Jessica Fusco, meet my brother. Nick, meet Jessica."

Making a formal bow, Nick said, "I'm honored."

Jessica looked skeptical. "Brother? What brother?"

I guessed by the gleam in her eye what Alison was thinking: if Nick could fake a sister, why shouldn't she fake a brother? "Nick is one of the many delightful surprises my mother had up her sleeve," she said sweetly. "He lives in Mobile, Alabama."

37 ❦ Fall Frolics, Part II

A good thing happened: Jessica got mad. She thought Nick and Alison were making fun of her, and it affected her performance. She sashayed up to the front of the room with her nose in the air and scowled at her parents, who were right on her heels, armed with a camcorder. Then she started playing so fast that instead of water down the drain, "Reverie" sounded like a hoot owl with the hiccups. I liked it that way. So did Nick, who stamped his feet at the end.

"Is that good manners in 2094?" I asked.

He looked hurt. "It's not only good manners, it's classy! Most people just wave at the performer, but if you stamp your feet, it's more European."

"Even at live performances?"

"Live performances don't come to Glen Alcott," he said regretfully. "We have reciprovision."*

"Stamping tends to attract attention in our time," Bunny informed him. "You'd better clap like us, or Jessica might get the wrong idea."

So Nick clapped. I'm afraid Jessica got the wrong idea anyway, but it didn't matter because Fugleman struck up "Mending Wall, We Cherish Thee" and everyone but

---

* Reciprocal television. You stay in your own home, but you can interact with the performers. Since they can see you, there's a strict dress code. Like no watching from the tub.

Bunny stumbled out of the room. Why stumbled? Because we were reading the words off the back of the program. We're all familiar with the tune* but nobody, not even Fugleman himself, knows all five verses.

What about Bunny—didn't she leave the room? Of course she did! But she didn't stumble because she never bothers with the Mending Wall words. She just sings "Send in the Clowns."

* It's pirated from "Send in the Clowns."

38 ❧ Revenge of Fall Frolics

We ran into a little trouble once we were out on the grounds. The reason being that most people knew about Alison leaving. They kept coming up to tell her how sorry they were to see her go, but how thrilling it was that she was going to be a Curly Girl on TV,* and how nice it was that she could join her family in Mobile, Alabama. Except for Jessica, they were all willing to believe that Nick was her brother.

"From the back, you look a lot alike!" they'd say. Then they'd ask Nick what life was like in Mobile.

I told him not to answer, but Nick said he didn't mind. "If they're asking, it means they've never been there," he reasoned. "I can say anything I want, and they'll never know the difference."

Yeah, sure! He tells them that Mobile public schools have aquatic classrooms because students learn better while immersed in a saline solution—and they'll never know the difference?

"That's not even true about Glen Alcott, is it?" Bunny asked when we finally dragged him away from the crowd.

"No," Nick admitted. "We tried it, but the students kept falling asleep. One kid drowned."

---

* They looked at her kind of funny when they said it, though. Maybe because of the blue stripe down the side of her nose.

"Well, keep your mouth shut from now on," I said.

To be on the safe side, I took him on the nature walk two hours early. We came back in time for the three-legged race, which Nick and Alison won, by the way. Jason and Jessica came in second. I teamed up with Maple and came in last—she's so short that we just went around in circles.

39 ❧ Fall Frolics: The Bitter End

I guess that about wraps up Fall Frolics. The student-faculty tug-of-war was a farce, as usual.* And I'll spare you a description of the egg toss except to mention that Cathleen hard-boiled all the eggs on the sly so no one's clothes would get messed up. I wish she had warned me. If I'd known, I wouldn't have tossed my egg at Bunny. She claims it gave her a black eye.

---

* Every year the students pull the same trick: when the faculty is grunting and groaning and leaning way back, we let go of the rope. They fall for it every time! (Pun.)

40 ❦ Blue Monday, Black Eye

"I'm sorry, I just can't see it," I said.

Bunny tilted her head at another angle. "How about now? Just above the cheekbone on my right side."

"Sorry," I repeated. "It looks normal to me."

"Great!" she said. "First he gives me a black eye, then he says I look normal. You have to admit it's a lopsided kind of normal, at least."

"Should I throw an egg at the other one, too?" I asked.

Bunny didn't laugh. "Just peel it. Peel as many as you can, and throw out the ones that have gravel in them."

Monday is Bunny's day for cooking supper. Jason's too, but he had gone off to represent Mending Wall at a science fair, so he switched with me. Which is why I was making curried egg-toss casserole during study hall. There was an odd, sour smell in the kitchen; we were out of cream, so Bunny had made the sauce with Alison's yogurt instead.

"I'm not promising to eat this crap," I said.

"Don't, then."

I looked at her carefully. At her whole face, not just her supposed black eye. "What's wrong with you today?"

"Speak for yourself," said Bunny. "You're the one who's been insulting my eye and my egg-toss casserole."

"Okay," I said. "I'll start over. Come here to the window, where there's some decent light."

Decent was an exaggeration; it was pouring rain. But

Bunny walked over to the window, still holding a wooden spoon that dripped yogurt on the floor. "Well?"

"Well, you're right, I guess. There's a smudgy place just over the bone, and your skin looks kind of bruised.* Does it hurt when I touch it?"

"Not to speak of," she admitted.

"I apologize," I said. "I'm truly repentant."

Bunny tapped her forehead with the spoon, leaving a curry-colored smudge. "No blame."

"But about that casserole . . ." I went on.

"I don't plan to eat it either," said Bunny.

I assumed everything would be okay after that, but it wasn't. Bunny was fine so long as we were working on the casserole: slicing eggs and onions, and sprinkling cheese on top. But when we started on the salad, she got moody again.

"Have you noticed how weird everybody is acting recently?" she asked.

"Weird like how?"

"First of all, Jessica has been kind of bitchy, which she never used to be. Second of all, the way Alison carries on, you'd think she had swallowed a tray of ice cubes. Third of all, you're moody."

"Me moody? You're the one who's acting moody."

"So we both are. That's just what I mean."

---

* Not one word of this was true. All I noticed was that Bunny's eyes were the color of the scum that grows on ponds in spring (somewhere between brown and green), with dark flecks around the iris. Plus she had absolutely straight lashes. And nice skin, with one cute little zit on her chin.

"You and me and Jessica and Alison doesn't make everybody," I reasoned.

"It's everyone who has gotten involved with Nick in any way. Want to know what I think?"

"No, but I suppose you'll tell me all the same. What?"

"He's dangerous. Nick is."

It was the most ridiculous thing I had ever heard, and I told her so. She didn't listen to me, though. She just picked up a knife and whacked a tomato into little chunks. Then she started in on a defenseless carrot.

"Even if he doesn't do anything bad himself, he's a catalyst,"* she said when I had calmed down a bit. "Things were a lot calmer before he came. Hopefully, he won't come back again after Alison moves in with his family."

"She's not going to do that," I said. "I've decided it's a terrible idea, and I'm shocked at you for thinking of it. Alison is your friend, and you don't even *like* the future."

"Says who?"

"You said so yourself the first time we went there. You said, 'If this is the future, I don't like it.'"

Bunny shrugged. "That was then. This is now. Besides, it's not your decision. Obviously Alison would be happier in the twenty-first century. No mom, no Curly Girl, no Mobile, Alabama."

"Oh, yeah? How do you plan to wipe Mobile off the map?"

"I'm serious, Jericho. Alison is a case of arrested development. Her mom has tried so hard to turn her into a Curly

---

* *Catalyst* is a fancy word for something that provokes a change in something else. Bunny was showing off. She was also wrong.

Girl that she's made her scared of growing up to be a woman."

"Bull!" I said.

"No bull. Face it—Alison will never grow up at all if she doesn't get out in real life with a real family and warm up a little. Mending Wall is a dead end for her, and she's a dead end for you. Think about it!"

"Don't tell me what to think about," I said.

Bunny took some plates out of a cupboard and slammed them down on the kitchen table. I didn't offer to help.

41 ❦ Confronting Fugleman

When Bunny starts slamming things around, it's best to leave her alone for a while, so I didn't hang out in the kitchen to discuss the matter. Instead, I set off to confront my father.

Wouldn't you know it, Fugleman was on the phone again. "Yes, what is it, Jericho?" he asked, cupping his hand over the mouthpiece.

"Two things," I said. "First, I want you to let Alison live full-time at Mending Wall until she graduates. Second, I want you to go to court and get the judge to appoint you as her legal guardian."

He said, "I'm busy, Jericho."

If you think I gave up, you're wrong. I sat down on the special straight-backed chair where he puts kids that need talking to, while he tried to convince an official at the science fair that there was no need to report Jason's project* to the ASPCA.

"Now, what's this nonsense?" he demanded once he got through with the official.

"Alison should stay here," I said.

"Forgive me if I'm wrong, but haven't we already dealt with this?" Fugleman asked with a warning look in his eye.

---

* Jason had trained a goat to work a treadmill that generated enough electricity to work his mother's electric tweezers.

"We discussed it once, briefly. We haven't dealt with it, because Alison still needs us. There's no way you can call her mother a responsible parent, and Stanley Mifflin is worse, believe me. If he really cared about Alison,why did he wait fourteen years to show it?"

Fugleman breathed in deeply. Then he leaned forward, tilting his head and pursing his lips for a moment. When he spoke, it was with his slow patient-parent voice. "The point, Jericho, is that he's showing it now."

"A lot of good that'll do Alison!"

"Let's hope you're right," he said, deliberately misunderstanding me. "Adoption, in this case, is not a valid alternative."

Here's where I slipped up. I should have kept my proverbial cool, but for once I panicked. "There happens to be another alternative," I informed him angrily.

Fugleman raised an eyebrow. "Such as?"

"Such as if you don't adopt Alison, I'll marry her."

"This is not a joking matter, Jericho."

"Really?" I said. "Good you warned me. Alison and I might have laughed our way to Mexico."

He raised the other eyebrow. "Just out of curiosity, how does Alison feel about this—uh, alternative?"

He had me there, so I changed the subject. "It's not a choice between adoption and moving to Alabama," I warned him. "It's a choice between adoption and running away."

"Why do adolescents always exaggerate?" sighed Fugleman.

"Why do grown-ups always turn off their ears before they listen?" I asked.

I made a quick exit. Not because I was afraid he'd win the argument, but because I had thought of someone else who might adopt Alison. Who? Who but everybody's mama, the marshmallow, the people pleaser: Cathleen.

42 ❦ Confronting Cathleen

"How would you feel about adopting Alison?" I asked.

Cathleen was correcting Jason's math quiz. She motioned for me to be quiet until she finished, so I watched while she scribbled "Good! Good! Good!" all down the page.

"That last one's wrong," I said. "The answer should be seventeen *feet,* not inches."

"Jason got the procedure right," she argued. "That's what counts, isn't it?"

"Not out in the real world," I said.

Cathleen marked "100%" at the top of Jason's quiz and turned to me. "Now, what's this about Alison?"

"I asked how you'd feel about adopting her," I said.

Cathleen smiled. "Why do you ask?"

"So you'll do it, of course," I said. "She doesn't want to leave Mending Wall. If you adopt her, she can come to school with Zoë."

Still smiling, Cathleen shook her head. "From what I hear, Alison already has two perfectly good parents."

"Alison has two perfect jerks for parents," I argued. "It would be spiritual rape if she had to live with them, but no one seems to care. Everyone but me is standing back and allowing her life to be ruined."

The expression on Cathleen's face would have made me laugh if I hadn't been so angry. I could see her struggling with the concept of spiritual rape—trying to shape it into something that would please us all and keep us out of trouble.

"Your friendship has been a precious thing that will remain with Alison forever" is what she came up with.

I groaned. "Get real, Cathleen! You've got to help us. Alison will crack up if she moves to Mobile, Alabama. She's already cracking up just worrying about it. Haven't you noticed how withdrawn she's been lately?"

"Withdrawn?"

"Withdrawn," I repeated firmly. "Withdrawn, and introspective, and—well, cold!"

Cathleen looked doubtful. This time, she had to think hard to find the silver lining. She found it, though.

"Mobile, Alabama?" she said cheerfully. "That's near Florida, isn't it? Alison will be warm enough down there."

43 ❧ Confronting Alison

Alison gave me a cool-eyed stare. "What on earth made you think I'd want to be adopted?"

"So you could stay at Mending Wall, of course."

"That's not a good enough reason. Out of one dysfunctional family into another, is that what you're suggesting?"

"My family is not dysfunctional," I said stiffly.

"Your family is not a family," Alison corrected me. "Your mom walked out on you, right? She handed Maple over as if she were a package delivered to the wrong address, and you never heard from her again."

"So what?" I said. It wasn't a brilliant answer, but it was all I could think of.

"Was she ever married to Fugleman in the first place? And who is Zoë's father—does anyone know that? My point is, I don't need another non-family. I'd rather run away."

"Well, it's your problem," I said bitterly. "I just thought maybe there was some way I could help."

"There is," said Alison. "Next time, mind your own business."

44 ❧ To Prove that We're Still Friends

You think I gave up, don't you? You think my feelings were hurt and I went off in a huff. Well, think again. Sure, Alison had her bad moments. But there were other moments that made up for them. Here's an example.

It's still Monday, and it's still raining. School is almost over: just one period left. On Mondays, this period is devoted to Beneficial Motion, informally known to us students as BM. Depending on the weather, it can mean anything from volleyball to modern dance. Today Douglas brings down a bunch of old clothes from the attic and teaches a class in mime.

Get this straight: Douglas knows less than nothing about mime. But somehow he got the idea that if you make big, round eyes and scrunch your lips into a rosebud, you can reduce an audience to gales of laughter or puddles of tears. Only one problem: no audience. Fugleman hangs a Do Not Disturb sign on the study door. Cathleen has driven off to pick up Jason from the science fair. So seven kids act out the following for nobody at all:

1. Lifting invisible weights

2. Scolding an invisible dog for leaving an invisible mess on the floor

3. Saying good-bye to an invisible friend who is leaving you forever

Why only three choices? Because Douglas's imagination doesn't run to more. Those three are bad enough. If a stranger came by and looked in the window, he'd think this was an institution of a different kind.

Alison and I have made up by then, but we're both a little stressed out, so we sit on the floor and lean against the wall.

"Let's see some action, kids!" says Douglas.

There's white makeup on his cheeks,* and he's wearing a bowler hat. Alison gives him her chilliest blue-eyed stare.

"School isn't over yet," says Douglas.

"You may not like our act, but at least you could be supportive," says Alison.

Douglas doesn't quite dare ask what act. He suspects that Alison is pulling his leg, but he isn't sure. He hesitates. Then he falls for it. "I'm sorry, Alison," he says. "Which assignment were you doing?"

"We made up our own," says Alison. "We're watching invisible television."

"What's the show?" Douglas asks in this cutesy let's-pretend voice. "Judging by the lack of expression on your faces, it must be boring."

"Very boring," Alison agrees. "It's about mime. What do you say we change the channel, Jericho?"

I nod. Alison zaps the TV with her invisible remote control.

---

* Also on his moustache, so he looks as if he has been drinking a vanilla milk shake.

"Football!" she tells Douglas. "The Redskins are playing the White Sox."*

She roots for the Skins until class is over.

* Notice something wrong here? Good for you! Douglas didn't.

45 ❧ Playing Hooky

It rained again on Tuesday. I woke up to the steady pitter-patter of words against my ear.*

"Hark to the silent moaning of the sky!" BVD was murmuring.

I sat bolt upright in panic. "Huh? Whassa matter?"

"My soul is weary."

"BVD, are you okay?" I asked. "Should I call Fugle-man?"

He started over again:

> *Hark to the silent moaning of the sky!*
> *My soul is weary.*
> *Living is a dreary*
> *Business if you are I.*

"That rhymes," I warned him. "Wake up, BVD—you're having a bad dream."

BVD rolled over and buried his face in his pillow. "Or should it be 'if you are me'?" he asked in a muffled voice.

"I'd leave it the way it is," I advised him. "Otherwise you'd have to say, 'Hark to the silent moaning of the ski,' or some word like that."

---

* If you thought I was going to say "raindrops falling from the eaves," you're reading the wrong book.

"Don't be ridiculous," said BVD. "Whoever heard a ski moan silently? Why just one ski, anyway?"

"Make it a snowboard, then."

"Thanks for nothing! Can you think of a rhyme for snowboard?"

"So bored," I answered promptly. "As in, 'Life is a dreary business if you are so bored.' Which you wouldn't be if you developed an interest in girls."

BVD moaned audibly, got out of bed, and went to breakfast.* I stayed put for a while. The bell hadn't rung yet, so bed was as good a place as any to make plans. Alison was leaving on Saturday—just four days away. I wouldn't put it past her to run away, so maybe it was time to give Bunny's brilliant idea some serious consideration. As for solutions in our own time, I could think of only one more thing to try: talking to her mom. At the risk of being snubbed again, I decided to ask Alison for her mom's new number at breakfast.

Breakfast was banana pancakes that morning, with caprine sausage** on the side. I noticed that Alison was picking at her food. She had been picking at her food all week and was beginning to look thinner.

"Cheer up!" I said. "Trust your old pal Jericho and all will be well."

She looked doubtful. "What are you up to now?"

---

* That morning he emerged from under the covers in a dinner jacket and bow-tie. If BVD ever does become poet laureate of the United States, I could get rich writing his biography.

** Don't ask. Fugleman is responsible for breakfast at Mending Wall, and it's *always* safer not to ask.

"Be patient. Does your mom have a phone yet in Mobile?"

"Yes," she said.

"Can I have the number?"

"No," she said, standing up. "And in case you didn't know, cheering people up is an invasion of their privacy."

"When people are depressed, they need upbeat company," I said, and I stood up, too.

She pushed past me. "Excuse me, Jericho. As a matter of fact, company is the last thing I need. I'm going to cut classes this morning and take a long walk."

I felt suddenly alarmed. Why? Because Alison is not your athletic type. She likes to keep her body fit, but she would scorn the idea of taking it for a brisk hike in the pouring rain. She wouldn't even do that to a dog. Only something really important would get Alison outside in weather like that. Had she chosen this moment to run away?

"It's raining," I reminded her as I followed her out of the kitchen. "What's the point of running away in the rain? You'll just catch pneumonia and end up in a hospital."

"It may not be raining everywhere."

The light finally dawned on me. "Is Nick planning to cut classes, too?"

She shook her head. "He doesn't know I'm coming. I thought I'd check out Glen Alcott on my own. The town, I mean. Not just the Homestead."

"Give me time to change my clothes first," I said.

"What for? Nobody asked you to come."

"Tough! I'm coming anyway. Do you own anything that looks like a tunic?"

After talkfest, Alison went back to her room and returned with a sleeveless dress. As soon as we were alone in the kitchen, I pulled it on and stepped out of my jeans.*

"What about you?" I asked.

"I only own one dress," said Alison.

"Holy Moses! So borrow one from Jessica. Believe me, I'm not going like this if you're in jeans."

"I told you I didn't need company," said Alison.

Slipping off her shoes, she backed against the wall, and in spite of my threat, I followed. Unfortunately, we had forgotten Nick's advice and arrived just as the first tour of the Fugleman Homestead began, at nine o'clock. Already we could hear footsteps padding down the hall.

"This room has remained unchanged over the years,"** a pleasant female voice informed the visitors who filed into the kitchen a split second later.

"Hi, Lois!" said Alison.

I could have strangled her. Why draw attention to ourselves? After one look at the way Alison was dressed, Lois would teleophone to the USSB.

"You fool!" I said. "Quick, let's get out of here!"

It was too late. Lois reached out and grabbed her sleeve. Only guess what? They were both smiling.

"Good morning, sweetie. People, I'd like you to meet my assistant."

"Hi, people!" said Alison.

---

* Did I look silly? Of course I did. What a dumb question!

** What about that polished floor and the velvet ropes? What about Nick's name on the height chart? Grown-ups are the most incredible liars!

"My assistant is modeling typical late twentieth century informal wear," said Lois. "Boys' wear, of course—in those days, girls wore skirts. Turn around slowly, sweetheart, so we can see the tag on the right buttock."

To my amazement, Alison hitched up her sweatshirt and turned to display a leather tag that read LEVI STRAUSS.

"As you may have guessed, these trousers belonged to Levi Strauss," Lois explained. "Levi was not a member of the Fugleman Homestead, but the Fugleman boy-children would have dressed in a similar fashion."

"Were articles of clothing always marked with the owner's name that way?" asked a man with orange lipstick.

"I believe so," said Lois. "Let's move along so I can show you the quaint, old-fashioned sanitary facilities."

They moved along. So did we, and as soon as we were outside, I asked Alison what in the name of blame was going on. "Lois acted like you were old friends!" I said.

"We are," she agreed. "I've been here five times already. No, six, counting when I came with you and Bunny. I came during the soccer game, remember? And I came on Sunday after Fall Frolics, and twice yesterday, and at six o'clock this morning. When there's a tour group, I model the old clothes for Lois. These jeans are mine, of course, but she can't tell the difference."

I was horrified. "You mean every time she calls you sweetheart, you turn around to show the tag on your right buttock? Why is that any less dumb than being a Curly Girl?"

"Because Lois wants me to model the way I am, not like some ditzy super-teen."

"Just where does she think you come from?"

"She thinks I'm playing hooky from Glen Alcott Junior High, but she doesn't care."

"All the same, she must wonder," I said. "I mean, you don't talk like the other people here."

Alison shrugged. "I'm learning. Lois *needs* me, Jericho. She was a lonely woman before I came along."

It was either laugh or vomit, so I laughed. She refused to speak to me after that. We walked for hours without exchanging a word. The people we passed in the street kept pointing at her jeans, which didn't help things any. She didn't forgive me until we reached the end of town, at the Ammonoosuc River.* But on the way back, it was a different story; she had something nice to say about everything we saw. Cathleen would have been proud of her!

---

* The town on the far bank was Alcott Heights. The reason we turned back was that it looked just like Glen Alcott.

46 ❧ Confronting Mrs. Mifflin

"I'd like to speak with Mrs. Mifflin, please," I said.*

"This is Mrs. Mifflin," said the voice.

Only it was the wrong voice.

"Are you sure?" I asked.

"What is this? Who's calling, please?"

"Um—Mrs. Mifflin, this is Jericho," I said.

There was a pause. "Yes, Jericho?"

The problem was, the voice had a heavy southern accent. No way could Alison's mom have acquired an accent like that after just two weeks in Mobile, Alabama.

"You're not Alison's mom, are you?" I asked.

"No," she said. "I'm Stanley's mom."

"Well, can I speak to Alison's mom?"

"I'm sorry, she's not here. She and Stanley left on their honeymoon. Can I take a message?"

"I need to talk to her," I said. "It's kind of an emergency. Do you know where I can reach her?"

"They kept that a secret. All I know is, the three of them are showing up sometime Saturday."

"Three of them?" I repeated.

"That's right," she said. "They're bringing Alison back with them. Are you a friend of Alison's?"

---

* I didn't know whether they had tied the knot yet, but I figured there was no harm in pretending.

Before I could answer, she added, "She must be one excited little girl. Tell her not to worry—her mom got her into that charm school before she left. She's all signed up for the Saturday class, and another that meets three evenings a week."

"She'll love that," I said.

"What girl wouldn't? And tell her that her grandma can't wait to meet her."

"Yeah, sure," I said.

"And give her a hug for me, you hear?"

"Dream on!" I said, and I hung up.

47 ❦ Yin and Yang

When did the conversation with Stanley's mom take place, you're wondering. Why did I skip directly to it rather than say what happened when Alison and I got back from playing hooky?

I called from Fugleman's study that same afternoon. No one was in there for the moment, so I looked in Alison's file to see if by any chance her mom had sent the new phone number for Mobile, Alabama. Why was I alone in the study? What a lot of nosy questions! Because I was in deep scat, that's why. So deep that I was summoned to a Yin-Yang Session. But first, Fugleman and both mentors were having an informal conference about me out in the hall.

Yin-Yang Sessions are hot stuff at Mending Wall, so I'll give them a whole paragraph instead of just a footnote. In Chinese philosophy, yin stands for the somber, negative, and female qualities in nature, whereas yang stands for bright, positive, and male. Fugleman is forever explaining that you need both to be a normal person. It's by getting the balance wrong that you find yourself in deep scat. You can imagine Bunny's reaction to yin and yang when she first heard about them! But that's beside the point. The point that Tuesday afternoon was me.

A split second after I hung up on Stanley Mifflin's mom, they all walked in. Cathleen blushed, Douglas smiled a sad,

sad smile, and Fugleman asked me to please get out of his desk chair, but otherwise to sit wherever I liked. I stood.

"We're concerned about you, Jericho," my father said. "Not just because you opted to cut classes today, but because during the past week or so, your behavior has been irregular. Are you aware of the situations I'm alluding to?"

You've got to watch out for this kind of question in life. Depending on your answer, they call either a policeman or a shrink. In other words, it's a no-win.

"Could you define irregular?" I asked.

Fugleman gave me a humorless grin and said that rather than waste any more time, we'd start the Yin-Yang Session.

"Yin?" he inquired, glancing around the room.

Cathleen and Douglas looked uncomfortable. Not as if they were reluctant to complain about me—more as if they had so much to say that they didn't know where to begin.

"You can go first," Douglas told Cathleen.

"No, you," said Cathleen.

They ended up both talking at once. I won't bother to tell you who said what, because they interrupted each other so often that I can't remember. Here, in alphabetical order, are some of the yin words that stick in my mind. If you want to put them into sentences, be my guest—mix 'n' match!

Adolescent	Obsessive
Aggravating	Prepubescent
Attitude	Reprehensible
Behavior	Sex
Disappointment	Sporadic
Inappropriate	Self-defeating
Irresponsible	Uncouth

If you stop to look any of those up in the dictionary, you're a masochist.* Why not think about this instead: How come there's only one one-syllable word in that list? I was eager to think about it myself, but the whole point of Yin-Yang Sessions is that you don't give the victim time to think.

When the mentors ran out of steam, my father turned to me. "Well, Jericho?"

"Let's go on to yang," I suggested.

Douglas had to think hard before finding any yang. What he finally came up with was that my latest algebra quiz was an improvement over my second-to-latest algebra quiz, so maybe there was just the faintest hope of an upward trend. He tossed out a few yang words like *potential,* but then he got sidetracked on how I tried to cuddle** up to Alison in class. This was cheating; he's not supposed to let my yin contaminate my yang.

Fugleman cut him short. "Thank you, Douglas. Cathleen, have you anything to add to the yang side for Jericho?"

"Why, yes!" Cathleen said, treating me to her soppiest people-pleaser smile. "Jericho makes a very nice tuna casserole."

---

* There's a yin word they forgot! A masochist is a person who makes life hard for himself on purpose (in fact, it's the only easy thing that person does).

** I detest this word. It sounds like a whole slew of other words I happen to detest, such as *blubber, cud,* and *muddle.* Why not be honest and say I was trying to feel Alison up? She didn't cooperate, by the way.

48 ❦ Bunny and Butt-Brain

Bunny's eyes opened so wide that I could see white all the way around the pond-scum color. "I don't believe it."

"You don't believe what?" I asked.

"Boys!"

"Justify that remark," I said, hoping to beat her at her own game.

Her voice sounded hurt. "You and I were together when we discovered the future. It was like our thing. I call it downright sneaky and underhanded for you to go with Alison and not tell me."

"Sorry," I said. "I thought you'd be happy to hear how much she likes it there. You're the one who thinks she should move there permanently. She's been back five times alone already, and she's made friends with Fred and Lois. She's even beginning to sound like them. Personally, I think she'd be better off in Mobile."

Bunny said, "You would."

Where is Jericho now, you're asking. Still in Fugleman's study? Don't be dense! I left Fugleman's study as fast as my sporadic little legs would take me, after getting my yang-building* assignment. Which happened to be picking up litter left around the campus on Fall Frolics day. The rain had finally stopped, but not until it coated the litter with scenic New Hampshire mud. Fun, fun, fun!

Jericho wasn't the only one who played hooky, you're thinking. Shouldn't Alison have been Yin-Yanged, too?

Right! Only as soon as Alison realized she was in trouble, she disappeared again.

What's Bunny doing out there in the mud, you're wondering. She didn't do anything wrong.

True. I was wondering the same thing myself. My conclusion was that she came because she wanted to be with me. And yes, I was flattered. When you can't build your yang, build your ego—it feels just as good. Maybe better!

"Okay," said Bunny. "So Alison has problems with her mom, and the whole scenario sucks. That's still no excuse for leaving you to take the punishment. Where the heck is she, anyway?"

"Three guesses," I said. "You know what I can't get over? She really means it when she says Glen Alcott is a nice place to live."

Like I said, it had stopped raining. Bunny and I had worked our way up the slope behind our house, and we stopped for a breather just as a sunbeam reached through

---

* "Yang Builders are Mending Wall's answer to punishment. The student reinstates self-esteem through activities that make him or her aware of his or her role as a meaningful individual in our community." (A quote from one of Fugleman's newsletters to parents, in case you haven't guessed.)

the clouds and hit this old abandoned farm that we some-
times hike to, way off in the distance.

"You know what?" I said. "That's an inspiring view. I
never look out this window without feeling privileged."

Bunny caught the reference and laughed.

"Seriously," I said. "You won't find that in Glen Alcott.
No fields. No forests. No farms."

"If you don't watch it, you'll start sounding like BVD,"
said Bunny. But I knew she agreed.

"Alison likes farms," I said. "Not just Fisher-Price
farms—real ones, too. She likes animals. What does she
see in Glen Alcott? I don't get it!"

Bunny gave me a weird look. "Actually, there's this farm
in Glen Alcott."

"Yeah, sure."

"I mean it," she said. "It's about a mile beyond the
school. There's this sign that says how it's an exact replica
of New Hampshire's last remaining dairy farm.* They
charge admission."

"How do you know?" I asked.

"There was a supplementary insert in the brochure—
didn't you look at it? I got bored yesterday during study
hall, and there was no one in the kitchen, so I went for a
walk there."

"In the kitchen?"

"To Cow Land, butt-brain,"** said Bunny. "It was a nice
walk. I'd like to go back and visit there someday."

---

* In case you're wondering, New Hampshire's last dairy farm was in
  Monroe. It was zoned out of existence in 2009 when outraged citi-
  zens complained of the organic smell.
** See? She finally stopped saying Jerko!

"We could have gone today. I was in the kitchen during study hall. Helping you cook, remember? Why didn't you tell me you were going to the future so I could come, too?"

"You were acting too broody."

"I don't believe it!" I said disgustedly.

"You don't believe what?" asked Bunny.

"Girls."

"Justify that remark," said Bunny.

49 ❧ Every Litter Bit Helps

One time before a soccer match, I met this kid from Alcott Middle School who was scared—make that terrified—of Mending Wall. I knew it wasn't because of our brute force on the soccer field, so I chatted him up until I found out why. It turned out to be because of our lack of rules, believe it or not. According to him,* kids who share the same bathroom, plan the menus, go to class in their pajamas and recite poetry instead of the pledge of allegiance are lawless and a major threat to kids who don't.

If there's one thing I can't stand, it's when people start knocking our school. I mean, weird it may be, but scary it's not. So I rattled off this list of rules at Mending Wall: how we have to work in the garden and groom the goats, and how each senior has to teach a junior one new and interesting thing each day. The kid from Alcott Middle School kept backing away from me. When I got to the part about picking up litter as a Yang Builder, he couldn't take any more.

"What about detention?"

"What's that?" I asked.

"It's when they keep you after school as a punishment."

"What for?" I asked.

"It's a rule," he explained. "You do something wrong,

---

* Although I bet you dollars to doughnuts he was just quoting his mom and dad.

they get to keep you inside. But they don't get to make you pick up trash or anything perverted like that—that's probably against the law. Want me to report your father to the police? I could do it so he'd never know it was you who finked on him."

His offer came from the heart, so I refrained from violence. Instead, I told him that it was actually kind of fun picking up litter because of another rule at Mending Wall: anything good you find, you get to keep.

Bunny and I found a lot of pink programs on Tuesday afternoon, and dumped them into the recycling bin. Here's what we kept:

> A rhinestone earring
> Half a pack of Merit Ultra Lights
> A sodden copy of *Sweet Valley High,* volume 30*
> Three tennis balls
> A five-dollar bill

---

* Entitled *Jealous Lies.*

50 ❦ Return of Fall Frolics

As soon as Bunny told me about Cow Land, I was eager to check it out. But before I tell you about it, I'd like to backtrack for a moment. Remember that nature walk I took Nick on to keep him from telling more lies about Mobile, Alabama? Well, speaking of cows . . .

The juniors had set up the nature walk the day before Fall Frolics. With Cathleen's help, they tagged nearly two dozen types of trees, and as many shrubs and bushes. Each tag had a number, which corresponded to a name on this printed handout that was available to anyone who wanted to go on the walk. There was a second sheet with a description of any wildlife you were apt to see. I gave Nick a copy of both, but he just folded them and stuck them in his pocket.

"I know all that," he said politely. "We have to pass a test on local flora and fauna before we graduate from sixth grade."

"Okay, you tell me, then," I said.

He did. "Ironwood," he stated accurately, pointing at some sinewy gray branches. "Red maple. Shad bush, sumac, squirrel."

"Not bad!" I said. "What's that tree over there—number seventeen."

Nick barely gave it a glance. "Poplar, locally referred to as 'popple.'"

"Did you learn from books or something?" I asked. "It didn't look as if you had a whole lot of flora and fauna in Glen Alcott."

"There's a public arboretum in Alcott Heights," Nick explained.

A little later, we emerged from the wooded area and found ourselves at the edge of Floyd's lower field. Suddenly Nick froze.

"Bloody blame!" he said shakily.

When I saw what he was staring at, I laughed. "Don't worry—that's just a cow."

Taking cautious little steps, he moved backward to the shelter of a sugar maple. "I know it's a cow," he said testily. "A holstein heifer, to be exact. What's it doing loose in that field?"

"Eating grass?" I suggested.

"Shouldn't you report it to the authorities?"

When I looked at his face, I saw an expression of barely controlled panic. I didn't have the heart to tell him he was making a big fuss over nothing.

"I'll do that," I said. "Good you spotted it."

51 ❧ BVD Gets an Offer He Can't Refuse

Cows do not roam free—or even fenced—in 2094. Why not? Because there are no more dairy farms in New England, remember? The last people on record as having drunk animal milk were the members of the Grand Union. Cream and butter are things of the past.* You can buy half-ounce packages of farmer cheese in the gift shop at Cow Land, but they're intended as a joke; you're not expected to eat them.

Bunny and Alison and I didn't get a chance to visit Cow Land until Thursday, because the mentors were beginning to suspect something was up, so they kept a close watch on us. We were all three given yang-building assignments to keep us busy, such as putting up storm windows and rearranging a decade's worth of *National Geographic*s in chronological order. We even scrubbed the floors. Mending Wall hadn't looked so good for years.

On Thursday after school, they gave us a break. "Go for a walk," said Douglas. "Go climb a tree or something. Get lost."

Even then it wasn't so easy because BVD was in the kitchen making pasta.

---

* Don't panic—people get their cholesterol from other sources. In 2094, cholesterol is considered good for you. When you buy packaged food, the U.S. RDA percentage for cholesterol is always listed under Nutritional Information.

"Why are you doing that now?" I asked him. "Supper isn't for hours. I thought you were supposed to cook pasta at the last minute."

"You are," he agreed. "I'm just making the sauce ahead of time."

"Aren't you afraid of botulism?"*

"Not unless you spit in it."

"Would you like me to take over?" Bunny offered. "Cooking is a woman's job. You could go out and do something macho like split wood."

BVD gave her an incredulous look. Then he blushed and said, "Get lost."

Alison hitched herself up on the counter. "Funny, Douglas just told us that, too. Got any suggestions?"

BVD switched his incredulous look to Alison. So did I.

"How does a person *get* lost, anyway?" she went on. "I mean, you are where you are, philosophically speaking."

A distracted expression came over BVD's face. Bunny opened her mouth to protest, but I nudged her warningly; if BVD got inspired with a poem, there was a chance he might get lost himself.

"I see," I said. "Like, existence should be free of time and space."

"Hey, that scans!" said Alison. "Did you hear that, BVD? Listen: ex-*is*-tence *should* be *free* of *time* and *space*."

The sauce came to a boil and began rising toward the rim of the pot, but BVD didn't notice. "Iambic pentameter," he said thoughtfully. "Nice line, Jericho. Add thirteen more like that, and you'll have a sonnet."

---

* A disease you get from eating spoiled food. Beware!

"Not me," I said. "It's all yours."

"I'll be right back," said BVD, making for the door.

After he had gone, Bunny reached out and turned off the burner. "Nice job, Alison."

"Nice job yourself," said Alison. "You overdid it, is all. Next time say 'sensitive' instead of 'macho,' and he'll go for it."

"Dream on!" said Bunny.

52 ❦ A Hands-On Experience

It was 3:35 when we arrived at the Fugleman Homestead, but the three o'clock tour wasn't yet over. Lois was in the bathroom, showing the facilities to a group of school kids. I could hear her pleasant voice rising and falling as we padded past the open bathroom door.

"It was the custom for males to raise the seat," she was explaining. "Females left it in the horizontal position, symbolizing their role in society."

Bunny did an about-face. "That's a frigging lie!" she yelled, causing the school kids to jump about a foot in the air.

Lois had a big smile for Alison, but when she recognized Bunny,* she looked a little sour. It struck me that those two weren't made to get along, so I tried to pull Bunny away. It was too late.

"Children, here is my young assistant and two of her friends," Lois informed the group. "These young people are modeling typical late twentieth century informal wear. Alison's friend—what is your name, young lady?"

"Bunny," said Bunny, "and for your information, *young lady* is an outdated phrase, considered sexist and offensive by the late twentieth century."

---

* As far as I knew, they had only met that first time, when Bunny had said, "Search me!" and Lois had obligingly done so.

Lois ignored this outburst. "Bunny is an expert on antiquated bathroom fixtures. Am I correct, dear?"

"I seem to know more about toilets than you do, anyway," said Bunny.

"Children, we're in luck!" said Lois. "Bunny will now demonstrate the correct use of this facility."

Bunny fled. Alison and I followed her more sedately. All the way down the hall, we could hear the toilet flushing over and over as the school kids took turns pushing the handle.*

---

* Yes, I've seen and used a twenty-first century toilet, but if you seriously think I'm going to describe it, you can seriously think again. Be my guest—let your imagination run wild.

she was going off duty. Only when she pulled her wig off, I realized she was a milk*man*.* He really hustled us along, so I didn't have time to see all the exhibits on the way back to the exit. Here are a few of them, though:

(One hen—in a locked glass case on a Styrofoam nest)
Label: *Hen. Parental Guidance Recommended.*

(A Yamaha snowmobile)
Label: *Manure Spreader, Circa 1940:*
    Found in Abandoned Shed

(A waterbed)
Label: *Supplementary Water Supply*
    For Use in Time of Severe Drought

(A John Deere tractor, 1950 model)
Label: *John Deere Tractor, 2001 Model*

(A Panasonic cassette player)
Label: *Primitive Communication Device*

(One cow, muzzled)
Label: *Dangerous. Do Not Tease!*

It makes you wonder about some of the stuff they tell you in museums in our time, doesn't it?

Nick bought us each a half-ounce package of farmer

---

* I should have guessed by all the makeup he was wearing.

cheese in the gift shop on our way out.* "So how did you like Cow Land?" he asked.

Rugged individualists we may be, but Mending Wall students are taught to have one thing in common: good manners when we go on field trips.

"Very nice," I said.

Bunny burped and added, "It was terminal!"

"This whole visit has been terminal," Alison said happily.

She spoke a little too soon; the visit wasn't over yet. When we got back to the Fugleman Homestead, Fred and Lois grabbed us and insisted on giving us a snack. It wouldn't have been polite to refuse.

* Bunny ate hers, attracting quite a crowd.

54 ❧ Sea-Whiz and Other Goodies

When I made that list of nice things about Glen Alcott, I should have added bread. It was fantastic bread: yeasty and crusty, and you could eat as much as you wanted without regretting it later. What's more, it was one of the few foods left that weren't produced through transpropagation. I asked Lois for the recipe, but it turned out you needed a macrowave oven,* so I didn't write it down.

"This is the best bread I've ever eaten," Bunny announced, stuffing a third slice into her mouth. "I'll have some more of that green drink, too, if you don't mind. It's truly terminal. What's it called?"

Lois passed the green drink, which was in a pitcher and tasted as if it had something exotic like crushed kiwis in it. "That's Sea-Whiz. I can't believe you don't drink it at home. Are your parents algaphobes?"

"Huh?" said Bunny, her glass halfway to her mouth.

"Algaphobes," Lois repeated. "Part of that new group

---

* *Macrowaving* means your entire kitchen space is programmed to cook food. You leave the bread or whatever on the counter, go out, and throw a few switches—checking first that the cat isn't asleep in some quiet corner.

that objects to flooding the market with algae derivatives."

Lowering her glass, Bunny stared thoughtfully at it for a moment. Then she raised it to her mouth again and drained it. As I said before, Bunny has guts.

Lois was smiling at her now. I was glad they were on better terms, and for the first time in all my visits to the future, I began to relax. It was already pretty dark outside. Off in the distance, we could see millions of tiny lights: people were eating supper in the Glen Alcott condos. We were late for our own supper, but I didn't say anything because we were having fun.* All of us. It was the first time I had seen Alison look happy for days.

"I hear congratulations are in order," Alison said, beaming at Fred. "According to Nick, that marriage renewal test is really hard!"

"It's a piece of cake with a hubby like mine," Lois said, winking flirtatiously at Fred. "I'm lucky, though. Some wives claim it gets harder every time."

Fred reached across the table for her hand. Personally, I was tempted to barf.

"You guys are wonderful," said Alison. "My mom would flunk straight off. There's no way she'd pass a test for marriage, to say nothing of parenthood. If they wanted my mom to pass a test for parenthood, it would take them six weeks just to find her."

---

* Were you thinking we couldn't leave anyway until we were alone in the kitchen? Wrong. The original kitchen was an exhibit, remember? The macrowave kitchen had been installed for the caretakers in what used to be my father's study.

"If she'd had to pass one before having you, you might never have been born," I pointed out.

"That's better than being a Curly Girl," said Alison.

"What's a Curly Girl?" Fred asked, and when we explained, he was shocked. "I assume this is a joke," he said primly. "An imprudent one, in my opinion, since it could get your mother in trouble. Beauty salons are illegal."

"No kidding!" said Alison. Naturally, she was delighted. "But if beauty salons are illegal, how come all you guys wear makeup?"

Fred gave her a weird look, and I couldn't blame him. He still didn't know we were from his past, remember. Neither did Lois. "Every schoolchild in Glen Alcott knows the answer to that," he said. "Maybe every schoolchild in the whole United States."

"I'm absent a lot," said Alison. "There are like these gaps in my education."

"But the children who remain at home have been proved to be *better* educated!" he protested. "Due to the fact that they can watch more television, you know."

It was obvious that he was becoming suspicious. Nevertheless, he told us how for half a century, makeup had come into the category of substance abuse, but then the hemancipation movement had fought for the right for men to wear it anyway.

"How come men and not women?" Bunny asked. "That's awfully sexist, isn't it?"

Fred blotted his lipstick on a paper napkin and stared at us with narrowed eyes. It struck me that it might be a good time to change the subject, so I asked *him* another question.

It was a conventional question—not worthy of my Mending Wall education*—but I was tired, okay?

After I asked it, Lois stopped smiling. Fred turned pale under his makeup and glanced toward the window as if someone were spying on us out there. Nick groaned and clapped his hand to his forehead. Want to know what the question was? You're in for a treat. Here goes:

"So who would you say is going to be your next president?" asks Jericho.

---

* Fugleman says that in conversation, we should always try to take the road less traveled by. You guessed it—that's from yet another poem by Robert Frost.

55 ❧ The *P* Word

I've said the wrong thing once or twice in my life. Many times, to tell the truth. So I'm familiar with what happens next. Namely, silence: an embarrassed silence, or an angry silence, or maybe an icy silence, which is the worst kind of all. That evening when I said the *P* word, I got a mixture of the three. Uh-oh! I thought. You've put your foot in it again, Jericho.

I didn't know about the *P* word yet, so I couldn't even apologize. "Hey, guys!" I said. "Clue me in—did I say something wrong?"

Fred went over to the window and looked outside before drawing the curtains. Then he turned and spoke in a low-ered voice. "You'd better go ahead and tell them, Nick. We wouldn't want them asking some stranger the same thing and getting into trouble. But after that, we have some questions of our own."

So Nick told us. Apparently, the United States of America had been without an executive leader since 2072, when the last of our presidents did something unspeakable.

"Like what, for instance?" Bunny asked.

"Oh, my!" said Lois, looking helplessly at Nick.

Even Nick looked uncomfortable. "I did a social studies paper on p—on the executive branch of the federal govern-ment—just last month."

"So?"

"So I know about it. What happened is, starting in the mid–twentieth century, candidates for p—I mean, for the chief executive office—came to have less and less personality. That's because whenever one of them had an outstanding feature, some political group or other would object to it. Pretty soon, the winners had no personality at all. As a result, they were given less and less authority to act."

"That makes sense," I said.

"Not really," said Nick. "By the mid–twenty-first century, these p—well, executives—"

Bunny interrupted. "President, president, president! Just say it, why don't you? Do you think we're going to wash your mouth out with soap?"

"Oh, please!" said Lois.

But Nick took a deep breath and said it. "By 2050, the . . . president had become such a nonentity that in a nationwide poll, seventy-eight percent of Americans didn't recognize his photograph."

"This made him dangerous?" asked Alison.

"Not that particular one," said Nick. "He was only potentially dangerous. You see, being nonentities and having so little power, the presidents got bored. They tended to engage in undercover activities to help pass the time. The inevitable happened in 2072, when our last president got caught. He was impeached, of course."

"But wouldn't the vice-president take over?"

"Theoretically," Nick agreed. "Only problem, no one could remember who he was. So the speaker of the house stepped in. But at the next election, the position was abolished."

"Why?" asked Alison.

Nick shrugged. "No one voted."

"You're pulling my leg," I said. "How could the system function without a president?"

"Just fine," said Nick.

I didn't know whether to laugh or not. It was obvious that Lois didn't think he was being funny. She kept glancing anxiously at Fred, so I dropped the subject and asked what grade Nick got on his paper.

"C minus," Nick confessed. "My teacher said it was in poor taste."

"That's unfair," Alison said sympathetically. "And you still haven't told us what the guy did that was so shocking."

Nick hesitated. Then he whispered quickly: "He was a member of the Grand Union."*

I have to admit I laughed, and the laugh didn't go over too well. Fred had the look on his face that teachers get when they're about to drill you with a lot of questions, so it occurred to me that it might be time to leave.

"This has been really nice of you," I said, rising from my chair.

Bunny started to get up, too, but Fred motioned for her to sit down again. "One moment, please. I have a right to demand an explanation, don't you agree?"

Bunny's nose began to twitch; she never takes kindly to the word *demand.* "No. Why?"

---

* So who was the woman on the dollar bill? Her name was Staci Dunbar (possibly BVD's great-granddaughter), author of a best-seller called *Blamed If I Do!,* which definitively let the American public off the hook as far as assuming responsibility for their environment was concerned.

"Because you children are putting my family in a difficult position. Did you think we haven't noticed how often you visit the Homestead, and at what peculiar hours? Now, for reasons I won't bore you with, it would be awkward if the authorities became interested in which children are or aren't present at the Homestead—"

Alison interrupted him. "Nick told us about Rachel. Don't worry, we won't make trouble for you if you don't make trouble for us."

"But suppose people start asking questions? What should we tell them?"

"You could always tell them to mind their own business," Bunny suggested.

I kicked her foot under the table. To my surprise, she hooked her ankle over mine and left it there. This kind of distracted me, so I couldn't change the subject again, as I'd planned to do.

Fred smiled. "Seriously, one of these days, someone is going to want to know where you young people are from and how you got here. You don't act like typical Glen Alcott schoolchildren. Personally, I suspect you're runaways from an urban area."

An urban area? Us? For a moment I wished Fugleman were there to give Fred his famous lecture about *campus* meaning field. "Sorry," I said. "You couldn't be further off. We're every bit as local as you are yourselves. And my father is probably having a purple fit right now because we're not there for supper, so I honestly think it's time for us all to leave."

That's when Alison said, "Not me. I'm staying."

56 ❧ Rachel

"Way to go, Alison!" said Bunny.

I said, "Hold it, Alison. Let's not go overboard or anything. Let's give this some thought and get things back into proportion and weigh the consequences."

"I'm staying," said Alison. "The consequences of *not* staying are being a Curly Girl, and living with my mom, and no more Mending Wall. No, thanks! I don't know what the consequences of staying are, but I'm willing to risk them. If Fred and Lois will have me, that is."

"You're crazy! You don't just ask a couple to take on an extra kid," I told her. "Aside from the practical problems, there are some psychological factors involved and—"

"I won't be an extra kid," said Alison. "I'll be Rachel."

I appealed to Fred and Lois. "She's nuts, isn't she? Back me up—make her go home!"

You should have seen the gleam in their eyes. All their eyes: Fred's eyes, Lois's eyes, Alison's eyes, even Nick's eyes. I was looking at a bunch of happy campers.

"Give in, Jericho," said Bunny.

As she told me in chapter 40, it wasn't my decision. I didn't quite give in, but for the moment I gave up.

57 ❧ Confronting Maple

"Gotcha!" said Maple.

I nearly jumped out of my skin.

"I won't report you, though," she added sweetly.

Behind me, Bunny popped out of the wall. Maple didn't blink an eye.

"I knew you could do that," she said. "I've been spying on you, and I saw you do it twice before. Will you teach me?"

"No," I said.

Maple turned to Bunny. "You're supposed to teach me one new and interesting thing each day," she reminded her.*

"The square of the hypotenuse is equal to the sum of the squares of the opposite two sides," Bunny recited.

"I already knew that," said Maple.

"Listen, Maple," I said gently. "There are some things only big kids can do. Little kids aren't even supposed to know about them. If they so much as talk about them, they get into deep scat."

"I know about puberty, too," said Maple. "I also know how to keep my mouth shut, and I will. But you have to show me how to go through walls. Deal?"

* Fugleman's rule, remember? If we seniors stuck with it, Maple and Zoë would be the best-educated kids in the U.S.

"No deal," I said.

"Fugleman wants to know why you weren't here for supper," Maple warned us. "Alison missed supper, too. Was she with you?"

"None of your business," I said.

"I bet she's still on the other side of the wall," said Maple. "I want to go there, wherever it is. Show me how to do it."

"No way," I said.

But Bunny said, "If you promise to keep your mouth shut, you can come with us when we visit Alison."*

---

* I might as well warn you, this is a dead-end chapter. When Bunny tried to take Maple to Glen Alcott, it didn't work. You'll find out why at the end of this story.

58 ❦ Terminal Grits

Looking back, I realize we were incredibly lucky that Jessica and Maple were the only ones who caught us coming home from the future. Just think—Bunny and I had made four round trips apiece, and Alison had made eight and a half! I didn't stop to count my blessings on Thursday evening, though. I was too mad at Bunny.

"What the heck are you doing, letting Maple in on this?" I grumbled at breakfast the next morning. "Thanks a bunch for consulting me first!"

"You think you own the future?" Bunny asked. "What's wrong with letting your sister come along? I won't say it's a nice time to live, but it's a nice time to visit."

"I disagree," I said. "I happen to think it's a feculent* time to visit. If you take Maple, I'm going to take everyone I know there, so they can see what's going to happen if they don't watch out."

"You wouldn't be so stupid!"

"Try me," I said.

Maple came around the table to whisper a question in my ear. "Is that why Alison didn't come home last night? Because she slept over in the future?"

"Shut up and eat your grits," I said aloud.

---

* That's the word I used—no kidding. It's another useful one for letting off steam without getting into trouble.

A huge grin spread across Maple's face, but Fugleman frowned at me. *Shut up* is a bad swear at Mending Wall, where words like *feculent* slip by.

"Anything wrong, Jericho?" he asked.

"On the contrary," I said. "These are super grits, Fugleman. Aren't they, Maple?"

Maple said, "They're terminal!" With an impish glance at Bunny she added, "Want to know how I found out about *terminal?* I was hiding under your bed last Thursday while Nick was there."

No one had paid attention to our conversation up to then. Read it again and you'll agree that it wasn't particularly revealing apart from a reference to the future, and most Mending Wall students are bored silly by references to the future.* But when Maple mentioned Nick, Jessica's ears pricked up.

"Did I hear someone mention Nick?" she asked.

"Kindly drop the subject, Maple!" said Bunny.

Maple lowered her voice. "Why? You guys weren't doing anything wrong in there."

"No, but *you* were," said Bunny. "Honest people don't hide under beds."

"I was waiting for you to wake up and tell me my new and interesting thing for the day, but then Nick came in."

---

* Why? Because Fugleman keeps telling us how it's our responsibility, so we should aim at a better future each time we make a decision. He even put a poster in the bathroom saying "In the long run, men hit only what they aim at." The quote is from Henry David Thoreau, not Robert Frost. Bunny claims it's sexist, especially since it's hung above the toilet.

"Drop it!" Bunny repeated fiercely. "Can't you see Jessica is listening?"

"So what if she listens?" I said. "Calm down and quit acting paranoid."

"Where does paranoid come in? I'm being practical. Jessica couldn't keep a secret if you tied it to her with a ball and chain."

I think Jessica would have minded her own business if Bunny hadn't made that remark. But Bunny made it, and as a result, Jessica got all pink with spite and hurt feelings.

"Speaking of secrets," she said in a loud, clear voice. "What have you guys been whispering about—and where *is* Alison?"

59 ❧ BVD to the Rescue

I know what you're thinking. You're thinking Mending Wall is such a tiny school that a kid couldn't be missing without attracting a lot of attention. This is true. Ordinarily, if Alison hadn't turned up for breakfast, someone would have gone to dig her out of her room. But Alison had been in a foul mood all week, remember. Everyone assumed she was sulking because she had to leave Mending Wall on Saturday, so they were respecting her privacy. At least, that's my theory. But when Jessica asked where she was, Fugleman felt he had to do something.

"Anyone know where Alison is?" he asked.

For a while, no one answered. Maple kept the impish look on her face, but that wasn't unusual. Bunny kept her own face blank, and I made a big deal out of spooning some of those terminal grits into mine.

"Jericho?" asked Fugleman.

I shook my head, which could mean anything. Then I spooned in some more grits.

Unfortunately, Jessica was still feeling hurt and spiteful. "Funny, Alison was gone by the time I woke this morning, and her bed didn't look slept in," she said sweetly. Maybe she spent the night with her brother Nick."

"Brother?" Fugleman repeated in a mystified voice. "That's odd—there's no mention of siblings on her record."

"There's nothing wrong between Alison and her brother," Bunny said staunchly. "You're a snake, Jessica."

"And you're a liar," said Jessica.

My father may be lenient about the comings and goings at Mending Wall, but leniency has its limits. He told us that come to think of it, he *did* remember having seen someone in the back row with Alison when he was delivering his Fall Frolics convocation speech.* And hadn't Alison been wandering around that day in the company of a boy who looked an awful lot like her—from the back, at least? I affirmed that Nick really was Alison's brother. What else could I do, deny it? Maple, bless her recklessly loyal heart, told Jessica that she had a dirty mind. But it was BVD who saved us.

BVD had been studiously buttering an English muffin all the way to the extreme outer edge. He never took his eyes off it as he announced that Bunny was no liar, and he had known Nick for years.

"What?" we all asked in unison.

"Years," BVD repeated as he took a bite. In a muffled voice, he added. "Went to Boy Scout camp with him, summer of ninety-one."

For a moment, I believed him. I mean, the way he talked, it sounded really convincing. But then he ruined it by saying that they had been exchanging haikus by mail ever since. Ruined it for me, that is. Fugleman fell for it.

"Nick must be Stanley's son by a previous marriage,"

---

* So much for Bunny's theory that we could all strip naked and he wouldn't notice!

he said thoughtfully. "Or could he be another child born out of wedlock? In either case, here we have a classic example of a broken family. I'm glad it's finally being reunited."

"Well, maybe Nick isn't Alison's boyfriend, but he could still be Bunny's boyfriend," Jessica reasoned, but this time no one paid attention.

The whole thing blew my mind. Why would BVD speak out like that? I kept trying to figure it the whole rest of the way through breakfast. Reckless loyalty on the part of my little sister I could understand—but BVD? It didn't make sense. I tried to question him, but all he said was, "Chill out, Jericho."

So I dropped it. Not out of tact, or even the sheer hopelessness of getting an honest answer, but because something happened that wiped the whole incident out of my mind. Something gross. Something disastrous. Something terminal—to use the twentieth century meaning of the word for a change.

What, what, what? you're asking. I'm about to tell you, so get your imagination ready to paint another picture. Ready? Paint me at the breakfast table with my father, my sister, and the remaining seniors. Paint me full of grits. Paint me sleepy. But wake me up a little when I hear a car pull up the driveway. Got all that? Wait, there's more!

There is a lady in that car. She's getting out. Paint her green: green eye shadow, green jumpsuit, green high-heeled shoes, and a green tint to her bleached-blond hair. Add some jewelry. Go on, don't be shy. Add *lots* of jewelry.

You have to understand, this lady* dresses like a Christmas tree—all she needs is lights.

Okay, now paint her name in glitter across the page. What's her name? I'll give you a hint: she had changed it just a few days earlier.

* Bunny would like to go on record as objecting to this outdated, sexist word.

60 ❧ The Scat Hits the Fan

We don't get many visitors at Mending Wall, so we were all at the window in a flash. Including Fugleman, who didn't look exactly thrilled when he saw who had arrived. He hurried to the mud room to let her in, but then he hurried back in the other direction because he heard the front door open and shut. As I already told you, the front door is used so seldom that we forget it's there.

"I'd like to introduce Mrs. Stanley Mifflin," Fugleman said in this fake hearty voice when he came back with the Christmas tree. "Some of you knew Mrs. Mifflin when she was just Alison's mom."

Bunny looked nauseated. "Just Alison's mom, huh? What does that make you—just Jericho's dad?"

This feminist attack didn't affect Fugleman, who is used to Bunny, but it startled Mrs. Mifflin. "Don't I know you?" she asked nervously.

"Of course not," said Bunny. "I'm just your daughter's roommate. But that's okay, you probably wouldn't have recognized your daughter either. What the heck inspired you to show up here?"

"Bunny!" said Fugleman. I could tell there was a lot more he wanted to say, but he got choked up.

"Stanley and I decided to surprise Alison," Mrs. Mifflin explained with a Curly Girl smile. "We spent our honeymoon touring New England, so we thought we'd stop by the school."

I made a feeble attempt to smile back out of good manners. Not Bunny, though. She said, "Lucky Alison" in a voice that meant the opposite. Then we both glanced out the window toward where the car was parked, because we were curious about Alison's biological father. He wasn't out there.

"Stanley is waiting at the Maple Leaf Motel," Mrs. Mifflin explained when she saw where we were looking. "I thought I'd drive over and help Alison pack up her things. I know we're a day early, but Sunday is her birthday, and we're giving her a weekend in the Big Apple on the way south. Stanley promised to treat her to a whole wardrobe of trendy new clothes."

"She'll love that," Bunny said sweetly. "It'll be a consolation prize for fourteen years of neglect."

Fugleman made more choking noises and found his voice again. "Bunny, that's enough!"

"I'll say it's enough," Bunny agreed. "It's fourteen years too much, even. If Alison's mom wanted to give Alison a nice birthday present, she should have let her stay at Mending Wall."

I guess that's when Mrs. Mifflin wised up to the fact that her daughter wasn't there because she finally asked, "Where *is* Alison?"

Considering what a bind he was in, Fugleman sure came up with a cool remark. Want to hear it? Of course you do! Who knows, someday you may be the headmaster of a progressive school and have to think up something to say to the mother of a kid who has run away. Try this:

"Won't you take a seat, Mrs. Mifflin? Our mentors are about to arrive, and since this happens to be the scheduled time for talkfest, you might like to join us. Our first topic of discussion this morning will be Alison, who seems to have temporarily—uh—disappeared."

61 ❦ Enter Mervyn DeSoto

You may be wondering what I meant by *progressive* school. Don't bother to look it up. I meant that at Mending Wall we stress informality, individuality, and self-expression.* These things are okay on campus, but they don't always blend in with the community. In other words, what appeals to Mending Wall students doesn't necessarily make sense to parents or the police. Mrs. Mifflin didn't buy Fugleman's theory that Alison would come back under her own steam and be a better person for what he called "a learning experience." Mervyn DeSoto didn't buy it either.

Who is Mervyn DeSoto? I can't believe you've forgotten already. Better go back and read the footnote in chapter 1. That's where I first mentioned the police, remember? When a kid disappears, it's no joking matter. Alison's mom was on the phone within seconds of Fugleman's cool remark, and Sergeant DeSoto turned up ten minutes later. Meanwhile, the mentors had arrived: Douglas by himself, and Cathleen with Zoë. I knew it would be a humdinger of a talkfest.

Did Fugleman get right to the point? He did not. He didn't even introduce Sergeant DeSoto until we had all stood up and said, "Good fences make good neighbors."

* If you're still wondering why *progressive,* don't expect me to explain. Don't pin your hopes on the dictionary either.

DeSoto looked confused but must have guessed we were saying something solemn, because he tucked in his thumb and held four fingers to his brow as if it were the pledge of allegiance. For good measure he mumbled, "Amen."

I have to hand it to Fugleman. Instead of acting hassled, he took time to make two announcements. One was about vandalism in the barn* and the other about a rescheduled soccer match. I nearly applauded. When I'm that old, I hope I'm as good at keeping my cool. Then he paused, blew his nose on a filthy red bandana that he keeps in his pocket, and—finally—talked about Alison.

"Temporarily disappeared," he said. He had the phrase down pat by now, and it sounded more convincing. "Naturally I'm concerned," he told us, "which is why Sergeant DeSoto is helping me look into the matter. I expect you to give him your total cooperation. So if one of you has been keeping something back out of embarrassment or"— Fugleman glanced from face to face, stopping at mine a tad longer than at the others—"or out of some misguided notion of chivalry, now is the time to come clean."

No one came clean.

"Who was the last to see her?" he asked.

"Last I saw her was after supper," I answered truthfully. I didn't specify whose supper or what century.

"Where, Jericho?"

"Right here in the kitchen," I said, still truthfully.

---

* Someone had given one of the goats a facial. I swear! The poor thing was wearing lipstick, mascara, the works. Alison's Curly Girl kit was found behind a hay bale, but you're not going to tell me Alison snuck back from the future to abuse a goat. My money is on her mother.

They went around the room after that, asking where and when everyone had last seen Alison. Bunny's answer was the same as mine, of course. No progress was being made, so Fugleman asked whether any of us had noticed anything unusual lately.

"I'm not restricting that to Alison," he added. "I mean unusual activity of *any* sort at Mending Wall."

This was asking for trouble.* Naturally a bunch of people raised their hands. Douglas complained about the act Alison and I had put on during BM on Monday, and Cathleen brought up the mooning incident, and Jason mentioned the fact that Alison had had a red star on her chin when Mending Wall lost that game to the Rams. Jessica was the worst, though. She announced that about a week before Fall Frolics, she had seen me and Bunny come through the wall.

Fugleman stared at Jessica as if she had lost her marbles. "Through the wall?" he repeated. "What do you mean? Which wall?"

"Over there." Jessica pointed at the height chart.

In case you hadn't guessed, Jessica is kind of dim. No one took her seriously when she tried to explain, and she isn't the most self-confident person in the world, so I think she would have dropped the subject if Maple hadn't giggled.

"What's so funny?" Jessica demanded, blushing scarlet.

"You," said Maple. "It's funny to pretend you saw people

* Unusual activity is what Mending Wall is all about. Pay us a visit someday and show me an activity that isn't unusual.

coming through a wall. Funny-peculiar, too, not just funny-ha-ha."

"Oh, yeah?" said Jessica. "Well, there's something fishy going on, and I bet you're in on it."

Mrs. Mifflin rattled her bangles impatiently. "Even if no one knows where Alison went, do any of you have an idea *why* she might have gone?"

"Sure," Bunny answered with a dangerous glint in her eye. "She split when she found out she had to be a Curly Girl."

"She left the school," Fugleman corrected her.

"Split," Bunny repeated firmly. "Her mom wanted to turn her into one of those idiotic teenage bimbos, and Alison wasn't real happy. I'd split, too, if my mom did that to me. It's spiritual rape."

You should have seen the look she got from Mrs. Mifflin. It told Bunny that she was just about as low and ugly as a female human being can get, and that anyone who even dreamed of turning her into a Curly Girl would be wasting her money. But don't worry, Bunny gave her a look right back. The two looks might have led to an interesting discussion—the kind that gives our talkfests their well-deserved reputation—if Jessica had kept her mouth shut.

"I know nobody's interested in my opinion, but I'm going to tell you anyway," she whined. "I don't think it had anything to do with Curly Girls. I think Alison ran away with her so-called brother Nick."

"Her so-called what?" asked Mrs. Mifflin.

All of a sudden, I noticed a new tension in the kitchen. Sergeant DeSoto must have noticed, too, because that's when he took over. Stepping purposefully forward, he thanked us all. Then he said that rather than take any more valuable time away from our assembly, he and Mrs. Mifflin would question the seniors individually in my father's study.

62 ❧ The Naked Truth

Surprise, surprise—DeSoto picked on Jessica first! She was with him for a long, long time. At least, it seemed long to me and Bunny, who had been asked to wait out in the hall. When she came out again, she hurried past us, all hot-cheeked and self-righteous.

"Proud of yourself?" asked Bunny.

"You're next," Fugleman told Bunny, putting his head around the door.

"I don't mind going next," I offered gallantly.

"No rush," said Fugleman. "You'll have your turn."

"How about if we go in together?"

He didn't bother to answer that one—just ushered Bunny through the door and shut it behind her. She was in there even longer than Jessica, and I had no chance to question her when she came out. A pity, because I didn't want our stories to conflict. Not that there was much danger if she stuck to our agreement, which was to tell the naked truth.*

"Are you okay, Bunny?" I asked in passing.

"Jericho, please!" said Fugleman.

"Wait for me here," I said.

"I believe you're late for French, Bunny," said Fugleman.

---

* The truth about everything that happened in our time, that is. We assumed we wouldn't be questioned about the future.

You're wrong if you think I reminded him that there couldn't be a French class without him there to teach it. Why didn't I? Because he was looking a little gray around the gills by then, and I didn't want to make things worse. So I walked meekly into his study and sat down on—you guessed it—the straight-backed chair. I won't put you through the whole conversation. Only this:

DeSoto: What can you tell us about Nick?
Jericho: He's just this kid who's been hanging around Alison.
DeSoto: Have you ever noticed him in town or elsewhere outside of the school grounds?
Jericho: Uh—not this year.
DeSoto: (*Leaning forward eagerly*) Are you telling me that you remember seeing him in the past?
Jericho: No, I met him for the first time right here in school, a couple of weeks ago.
Mrs. Mifflin: What on earth led you to believe he was her brother?
Jericho: Well, you see, I wanted to believe it.
DeSoto: Why?
Jericho: Um—I was in love with Alison.

That session in Fugleman's study was pretty grueling. Not because DeSoto bullied me, but because I had to hold out on two unhappy people. Who? Well, Fugleman, for starters. He was carrying the weight of the world on his shoulders and looked about ready to drop it on his toes.

Who was the second unhappy person? DeSoto? You've got to be kidding! DeSoto was having a ball. No, it was Alison's mom. The whole time I was in there, she was crying. I wished Bunny hadn't shot her mouth off at her in talkfest. Believe it or not, I actually felt sorry for her.

63 ❧ The Fisher-Price Farm

They let me go.

Sure, Fugleman said things like, "Jericho, if there's anything you're holding back, for God's sake . . ."

There was, but I couldn't say it. Most of it he wouldn't believe anyway. In fact, I no longer knew what to believe myself. Mrs. Mifflin wasn't the only person I felt sorry for; I also felt sorry for *me*. It had finally struck me that I was the loser in all this. Why hadn't I forced Alison to come home? Why hadn't I told her that kids have survived worse moms than the one she was stuck with? Even as a Curly Girl in Mobile, Alabama, she would survive, and I might see her from time to time. But if she lived in the future, she could be dead as far as I was concerned.

In fact, Alison already seemed like someone who had died: someone who is real one day but the next day passes over into fiction. Like my mother, long ago. I remember, for a short while after my mother left, it seemed like she was hiding in another room of the house. But pretty soon I couldn't see her face inside my mind anymore. There was just a blank when I tried, and photographs were like illustrations for a story.

As I was leaving my father's study, I tried to see Alison's face inside my mind, to test myself. "Blue eyes, sharp features," I murmured. But it didn't work. Want to know whose face I kept seeing instead? Bunny's, that's whose. Not her actual face, which should have been right there waiting for me. No, what I saw in my mind was the face she tilted up at me that Monday after Fall Frolics when I hit her with the hard-boiled egg. I saw the pond-scum eyes with straight lashes and dark flecks around the iris. I saw the zit on her chin, even though it had been gone since Tuesday. But for the life of me, I couldn't see Alison. This really depressed me. How could I forget her face so soon? Chances were I'd never see her again, and I didn't even have a photo. Maybe Bunny had one, though.

"Where's Bunny?" I asked as I bumped into BVD.

"I'm looking for her, too. Isn't she in with your father and that policeman?"

"Her turn is over," I explained. "So's mine."

"Then I'm next," said BVD. "Did they give you the third degree?"

BVD looked truly rattled, so I reassured him. "Don't panic. They know you're not trying to hold out on them— they're just hoping for a clue."

"Well, they won't get one from me," said BVD. "Tell Bunny she can trust me. They can torture me if they like, but they won't get a thing out of me."

"What are you talking about?" I moved cautiously away from him. "Are you okay, BVD? You look kind of pale. Sure you're not going to barf on me or something?"

BVD glanced around with a guilty expression on his face. Then he handed me a piece of paper that looked as if it had been folded and unfolded about a million times. "Listen, when you see her, give her this for me. Okay?"

"What makes you think I'm going to see Alison?" I demanded.

"Alison?" BVD turned paler than ever. "Get real, Jericho!"

"Stop acting like a jerk and go in there," I advised him. "Otherwise they'll think *you're* the one who's holding out on them."

"They can stick pins under my fingernails," said BVD.

"Cute idea, but DeSoto doesn't seem the kinky type to me."

I opened the door to my father's study and shoved him through just as Mrs. Mifflin came out in the other direction. Things were getting worse and worse. Now I was alone with this woman, without even BVD to protect me.

"Hi," I said nervously.

Mrs. Mifflin blinked a few times, as if she couldn't really place me.

"Jericho," I reminded her. "I was just in there with you. Recognize me now?"

"Oh, yes," she said. "I'm sorry."

"No blame," I said, tapping my forehead.

She blinked some more. I hoped she wasn't going to start crying again. If she did, what should I do—escort her downstairs and let Cathleen take care of her? Maybe call Stanley at the Maple Leaf Motel?

Then she started shooting all these questions at me. Like why would Alison bother to run away when she was leaving Mending Wall for good anyway on Saturday, and why hadn't she let her mother know she wasn't happy here, and why didn't her friends *tell* someone so a session could be scheduled with the guidance counselor? The stuff Bunny told her in talkfest obviously hadn't sunk in at all.

"Mending Wall is too small to have a guidance counselor," I said. "Anyway, it wasn't the school that was the problem. Listen, you wouldn't happen to have a snapshot of Alison, would you?"

"That's what the policeman wanted, too. Luckily, I brought these."

Mrs. Mifflin had been lugging around this humongous shocking pink tote bag with "Curly Girl" printed on it. She set it down on the floor, poked around in it for a while and pulled out some computer paper, which she held so it unfolded in a long zigzag. What was printed on the paper? Alison's face times seven. Not the face I was trying to remember, though.

"That's not Alison," I said. "I meant, do you have a photograph."

"This is better," said Mrs. Mifflin. "This is what she's going to look like when I get through with her. It's all done by computer, see?"

I saw. Want to know *what* I saw? Lots of snaky hair that stuck out around Alison's head like that lady with real snakes in Greek mythology. Eyes that looked as if yours truly had been throwing hard-boiled eggs at them. Red lipstick. But no red star on the chin.

"This isn't going to be a big help to the police," I said. "Not to me either. I was kind of hoping you had a real photograph. Something I could maybe keep."

"You can keep this," said Mrs. Mifflin. "Go ahead, take a couple for your friends, too. I'll be printing out some more for the police to pass around."

That's when I gave up my illusions, short-lived as they

had been. I mean, it was like Alison's mom had never really seen Alison—not the way she was, anyway. She only saw her the way she wanted her to be. And if she really and truly wanted her back, it was only the computer-portrait Alison she wanted, not the real one.

"No, thanks," I said.

She tore one off anyway, and I was staring at it when Bunny finally turned up again. The real, noncomputer Bunny with her pond-scum eyes, no makeup, and that silly headband holding back her unpermed hair. She was out of breath from running, and she was holding Alison's Fisher-Price farm.

"Mrs. Mifflin already went downstairs," I told her.

"Good," said Bunny. "Are you through?"

"In more ways than one," I said.

"Then let's get moving. I take it the DeSoto jerk told you what he plans to do."

I shook my head.

"He picked up on Jessica's story," Bunny said, still panting to catch her breath. "About seeing you and me come out of the wall, and all. He's bringing in a team of forensic specialists."

"I don't even know what that is," I confessed.

"Experts," she explained. "Like in thrillers. They find the murderer by analyzing a hair in your soup."

"Quit fooling around, Bunny."

"Fingerprints," she said impatiently. "Stuff like that."

"So? They won't find much on the wall. Not in the crawl space either—just candy wrappers. If you're afraid they'll come out in 2094, forget it. That never worked for anyone but you and me and Nick and Alison. My theory is you have to be thirteen."*

"You may be right," said Bunny. "So even if she changed her mind, yesterday was Alison's last trip."

When I thought about it, I felt sick. "You mean she'll be fourteen on Sunday."

Bunny nodded. "Your birthday is in February, isn't it? Mine isn't until May. That gives me plenty of time to make up my mind. And chances are I won't move, because I get on fine with my parents, and I like this school, and—"

"And what? What are you getting at?"

"You," said Bunny. "I like you, too. But just in case I decide to live in 2094, I'm making a list of things to pack. Just in case I'm right and after I hit fourteen, I can't come back again."

If there had been a chair anywhere near where we were talking, I would have collapsed on it, because I felt as if someone had just punched me in the gut. In case she couldn't come back again? In case *Bunny* moved to 2094? That was crazy.

"That's crazy!" I said.

"No, it's not. I'll probably stay here, but I'm making a list, and you should make one, too. This might be the biggest decision you ever make in your life. What's the matter, don't you want to be where Alison is? I thought you were in love with her."

"So did I," I said, feeling my face turn red. "I mean, of

---

* Okay, so I wasn't thinking very hard. You probably have it figured out already, but you're not so emotionally involved.

course I am. But that doesn't mean I want to spend the rest of my life with her. I mean, in 2094. And you're not going to either—not if I have anything to do with it."

Bunny gave me a funny look. "Well, think about it, anyway. And meanwhile, you know what I want you to do?"

"Take this to Mrs. Mifflin," I suggested, reaching for the Fisher-Price farm.

I knew that wasn't what Bunny wanted, though. I had already guessed what she wanted me to do, and when she wanted me to do it: right that very minute, while DeSoto was still in Fugleman's study.

"Okay," I agreed. "But you come, too."

64 ❧ Maple Screams

I know what you're thinking. You're thinking we had no proof whatsoever that you had to be thirteen to go back and forth to the future. Just because it didn't work for Maple didn't mean it wouldn't work for Alison after Sunday, or that she and Nick could never visit us again. And you're probably right, but I wasn't taking any chances.

"It's nearly three o'clock," I said, checking my watch. "We can just make it before the tour gets started if we leave right now."

It wasn't easy. A bunch of people were hanging around the kitchen—kids and grown-ups—and Cathleen was dealing out mugs of herb tea. We had to ask Maple to help us.

"Go out to the mud room and scream," Bunny whispered, drawing her aside for a moment.

"What for?" asked Maple.

"To get everyone out of here. Jericho and I need to be alone in here for a minute."

"To do what—play with cows and horses?" Narrowing her eyes, Maple glanced down at the farm, which was swinging from the handle on its roof. "How about if Zoë screams, and I come with you to see Alison?"

"Who said anything about Alison?"

My sister said, "Get real, Jericho!"

"You know you can't come," I told her. "You already tried, remember? You have to be thirteen to do it."

"Like all the other fun things," Maple grumbled, but she headed for the mud room.

"Hold it!" Bunny said. "You better make it realistic. Use your imagination. Because I want it to work again when you do a repeat performance two hours from now. Five o'clock on the dot, okay?"

"Okay, but you owe me," said Maple.

It didn't take her long to reach the mud room. Before I had time to put my fingers in my ears, she let out a realistic, highly imaginative, blood-curdling scream.*

---

* Want to know what she said when they came running? She said she looked out the window and saw Alison. She said the same thing two hours later, but no one fell for it. It got them out of the kitchen, though, which was all that mattered.

65 ❧ Alison Chills Out

Once we were alone in the kitchen, we moved fast. Bunny backed up against the height chart, and a moment later, I did, too. Time travel was old hat to us now—like biking into town. When we were both at the Homestead, we ran upstairs to Nick's room, hoping to find him and Alison. They weren't there, though. On our way down again, we met Fred.

"Shoes off," he said automatically.

"Where's Nick?" I asked.

"He isn't back from school yet."

"Have you seen Alison?"

"Rachel is taking a group around. She knows the ropes by now, so Lois took the afternoon off to do some shopping."

Bunny did a kind of dance as she kicked off first one sneaker and then the other. "This I've got to see!" she gasped. "Which room have they gotten to?"

Fred didn't need to answer, because suddenly we heard Alison's voice. That is, a voice that sounded as if Alison had taken lessons from a talk show moderator. "Females left it in the horizontal position, symbolizing their role in society," she explained to a captive audience in the bathroom. Then, recognizing us, "These two young people are modeling typical late twentieth century informal wear."

"These two young people need to talk to you," I said. "In private."

There was a flicker of interest in Alison's eyes when she saw the Fisher-Price farm, but she went on with her job. "Informal wear for males, that is. To be historically correct, the young lady should be wearing a skirt."

"Chill out!" said Bunny. She stared in horror at Alison's red cap with a badge on the visor, and her red tunic with gold buttons.

"This young man's trousers belonged to Levi Strauss. Turn around slowly, Jericho, so we can all see the tag on the right buttock."

"Take a few minutes off," I pleaded. "I've got a note for you from BVD, and listen, could you at least meet us by the bridge after the Homestead closes?"

"Levi was not a member of the Fugleman Homestead, but the Fugleman children dressed in a similar fashion. Turn around, Jericho."

The visitors were beginning to look impatient, so I turned. "I think you should change your mind about staying here," I said, feeling slightly dizzy.

Alison said, "Get real, Jericho."

66 ❧ Jericho Gets Real

We had over an hour to kill. Feeling kind of gloomy, Bunny and I walked down the field to the brook, where we stood resting our elbows on the little iron bridge.

"She's beginning to change," I said. "Did you notice how cold she acted?"

"She was always kind of cold," said Bunny. "Where's that note from BVD? Let's find out what it says."

"But it might be personal!" I objected.

"He didn't say so, did he?"

Taking it from me, she opened it. I was right about personal. Only it wasn't for Alison.

LOVE SONG
by Bartolomeo Vanzetti Dunbar

B eauty, they say, is no deeper than the skin.
U nder your skin, you are still beautiful.
N ow, as a poet, I would be undutiful
N ot to point out the crystal truth therein:
Y our soul and body, through and through, are skin.

Believe me, I was flabbergasted. Bunny? That note was for Bunny? I tried to remember the stuff BVD had said outside Fugleman's study, about how we could trust him, and he wouldn't talk even if he was tortured. All that was to protect Bunny—not Alison?

"Well, gag me with a goat!" I said.

Bunny blushed, believe it or not. "It's a poem, Jericho. Written just for me. BVD is so sweet and old-fashioned!"

"Are you kidding?" I asked. "The guy says you're nothing but one big hunk of epidermis, and you think he's sweet and old-fashioned? He's gross is what he is. Did you notice that that poem rhymes? BVD is in real trouble when his poems rhyme."

"Stop being so goddamn cynical!"

"Sorry," I said. "It's just I don't get it. BVD isn't in love with you. BVD has never been in love with anyone."

Bunny raised her eyebrows. "Get real, Jericho!"

"Get real yourself. I'm his roommate, right? I should know. BVD's heart beats in iambic pentameter. He dreams about the centerfold in *New England Quarterly.** He doesn't know one end of a girl from the other."

"Do you?" asked Bunny.

I reached out to demonstrate, but she was too quick for me.

"You think you've got everyone figured out, don't you!" she said, darting over to the other railing. "When was the last time you updated us?"

"Who needs updating?"

She smiled. "Think about it. Make your own list."

Ordinarily I object to being told what to think about.** But as I said, we had time to kill. And it was a fact that

---

* Want to know what that is? I'm not telling. But if you've begun to drool, either you're BVD or you have a dirty mind.

** Okay, I'm aware that I've told you what to think about the whole way through this story, but that's different.

certain important people in this story had acted out of character—out of the character I assigned them, at least. So I made a mental list, starting with BVD.

1. I had to admit, it looked as if BVD was in love with Bunny. This proved I didn't know him as well as I thought I did. Plus it explained why he defended her when Jessica called her a liar.

2. Alison's mom couldn't be all bad if she cried when she lost Alison. And here's something to chew over: if Alison's mom waited fourteen years to let on that Stanley was her father, maybe she waited to tell Stanley, too. In which case, he was less at fault.

3. Jessica, on the other hand, came out worse than I led you to believe back in chapter 17. Good, all-around citizen of Mending Wall? Give me a break!

4. What about Alison—was she still my best friend? She had grown so distant in the past two weeks that I hardly knew her anymore. When that happens to a friend, you wonder how well you knew her in the first place.

This was heavy stuff! I heaved a big sigh and looked reproachfully at Bunny. She was dropping twigs over her side of the bridge and then running to the other side to see which one went faster down the brook.* Little wisps of hair blew around her ears and she kept biting her lip with this concentrated expression on her face. I realized that I was really glad she was there.

"Who's winning?" I asked.

"Me," Bunny said, dropping two more twigs into the water. "I'm the winner every time."

"Isn't it cheating to win every time when you play against yourself?" I asked, to tease her.

Bunny stuck her chin out defiantly. "I should play against myself and be the loser?"

> 5. Bunny. It struck me that she wasn't a single bit like Alison. And then this recklessly disloyal voice inside me said, "Good!"

"How are you doing with that list?" Bunny asked.

"Okay," I said. "I've updated five people so far: BVD, Alison's mom, Jessica, Alison, and you. Got any more suggestions?"

"Here's one," said Bunny.

She proceeded to tell me about another person who had changed. Not just who—also why. So I made a final addition to my list:

> 6. Jericho.**

* This game is called Poohsticks. I know because Fugleman used to read *Winnie-the-Pooh* aloud to me—way, way back before I knew there was a girl named Bunny.

** I'm not going to waste time explaining how I've changed. Update me yourself if you like—be my guest.

67 ❦ Jericho Grows

Alison was late. It wasn't until 4:30 that we saw her come out the mud room door and start down the field, still dressed in her tour guide's red cap and tunic.

"What took you so long?" I asked when she joined us.

"Souvenir T-shirts,"* she explained, taking off the cap and fanning her face. "I sell a lot of them to the visitors. Lois used to do it, but she was really overworked until I came. She says she doesn't know how she got along without a daughter. I don't know either."

"Listen, Alison, you're making a big mistake," I said. "Lois is okay, but she's not your mom. You should have seen how your real mom cried when she found out you ran away!"

"Call me Rachel," said Alison.

"Honestly, I think she really cares about you."

"It's not me she cares about—it's a Curly Girl."

"Isn't that better than a mom who makes you dress in a dumb tour guide uniform?

"No."

"You're making a mistake," I repeated. "I bet you could work things out with your mom. I bet if you sat down and

* The printing read: "My Parents Visited the Fugleman Homestead and All They Brought Me Back Was This Lousy T-Shirt."

explained how you feel, you could reach some kind of compromise, and after a while you'd grow to love and trust each other."

"Barf," said Alison.

I tried another angle. "You never know—Mobile, Alabama, might be fun. More fun than Glen Alcott, anyway. Do you really want to live in a time where everything is so much the same that no one bothers to travel?"

"Yes," said Alison.

"And crowded!" I went on. "There are too many people in the future. Look around you. See anywhere except the campus where there aren't any buildings? And this is a rural area! It's too quiet for a rural area. No animals, for one thing. I thought you loved animals!"

"They're getting another cow for Cow Land," Alison said defensively. "Fred saw it on the news. It was born in the Boston zoo, and Glen Alcott was really lucky to get it."

"Hot diggety dog!" I said. "That's going to make life a lot nicer for you, isn't it!"

"Yes," she said. "Fred says now that there are two, they'll need someone else to help exercise them. I thought I'd apply for the job."

"You mean saddle them up and ride them around town? You're nuts! Make her see reason, Bunny."

Bunny said, "It's your life, Alison."

Flashing her a sudden smile, Alison said, "Crimeny, Jericho! It's Bunny you should be in love with, not me."

I quit arguing. Besides, it was almost five o'clock, and if Bunny and I didn't coordinate our return with Maple's second scream, we'd be in deep scat. So I gave Alison a hug before she could protest,* and we all ran back up the field to the Fugleman Homestead.

"Quick!" Bunny panted as we hurried into the kitchen. "By my watch, we're already a minute late."

I was the first to slip under the red velvet rope and back against the height chart, but nothing happened. "It's not working," I told her.

"Here, let me try." She pushed me out of the way, took my place, and promptly disappeared.

"Holy Moses!" I said. "Now what do I do?"

"Try again," said Alison.

I tried again. Still nothing happened. Except that all at once, my whole body went numb and cold with panic.

"Scat!" I said.

"Calm down," said Alison. "Maybe it's not working because you care too much."

I gave her a startled glance. "Care about what?"

"About going home. Admit it—you'd rather never see me again than get stuck in 2094."

"I won't be able to come here anyway, once I'm fourteen," I told her. "Starting Sunday, you can't come back to our time either."

"What are you talking about?" she asked.

"Sunday is your birthday, remember? The transvector gate, or whatever—it only works if you're thirteen."

Alison laughed. "You've got it all wrong. Jason and Jessica are thirteen, too, so how come they never got here?"

---

* It was like hugging a coat rack but I could tell she wasn't indifferent to me because afterward, her eyes were aqua.

"I don't know," I admitted.

"Well, I *do* know," said Alison. "It's how tall we are that counts. You and I and Nick and Bunny were all the same height for a while, remember? It isn't a transvector gate, it's just a transvector *line*. Try scrunching down—I think the problem is that you grew."

"I'm going to miss you," I said as I scrunched down.

This time it worked.

68 🌺 Floyd's Field

Obviously that wasn't the last of it. The police investigation went on. And on, and on. The forensic experts came and went.* So did a bunch of cops whose names I can't remember. I'm not going to tell you about any of that stuff. But I thought I'd share a conversation I overheard between DeSoto and Fugleman when I happened to be outside my father's study.

DeSoto: Nice view you've got here.
Fugleman: It's an inspiring view. I never look out this window without feeling privileged.
DeSoto: Better enjoy it while you can. Soon as the ground thaws next spring, you'll be seeing bulldozers out there instead of cows.
Fugleman: What do you mean?
DeSoto: Floyd sold his field—didn't you hear? Some developers are moving in with a low-income housing project.
Fugleman: The day that happens, I'll pack up the

---

* They found Alison's fingerprints in the crawl space, among a bunch of others. They found candy wrappers, too. Also what they assumed was a joint, but turned out to be fish food wrapped in tracing paper. You never know at Mending Wall!

	school and move north. It'll never get by the zoning commission, though.
DeSoto:	Better start packing, because it already got by. They even chose a name for it. Glen—Glen something or other.
Jericho:	Glen Alcott?
Fugleman:	Go back to class, Jericho.

69 ❧ Yinfinity

Now you know everything. Unless you're curious about me and Bunny, which is really none of your business.

Did we ever return to 2094? We did not. No one else did either, because Bunny scraped the height chart off the wall. Fugleman didn't like her attitude during the police investigation, so he called a Yin-Yang Session and gave her a yang-building assignment of cleaning the kitchen wall. He never told her to remove the height chart, though, and he had a purple fit when he saw that it was gone. I wasn't too happy either.

"Why did you do that?" I asked Bunny.

"Because we're not the only ones at Mending Wall who grow. You wouldn't want to leave it here as a booby trap for one of the juniors who couldn't handle it as well as we did."

"You're the one who was going to bring Maple," I reminded her. "That shows you thought *she* could handle it."

"Well, maybe she could," Bunny admitted, "but I had another reason, too. Do you realize what would happen if people in 2094 found out that kids who were five-foot-five could travel to our time?"

"What?" I asked.

"Their parents would send them, that's what. By the millions. They'd solve their overpopulation problem by sending their kids to colonize the past."

"Very funny," I said, but I knew it wasn't.

I told her she should have asked me first about the height chart, but I didn't make a big deal of it. Why bother? It was too late anyway.

Here's what I'd like to know: does it mean none of this ever happened? If there's no more height chart in 1994, there wouldn't have been one in 2094 either, so Nick couldn't have come here. But he did, and we went there, and what's more, the height chart in the kitchen of the Fugleman Homestead showed that I grew. My theory, for what it's worth, is that all time is coexistent. Chew that one over.

And while you're at it, see if you can answer this: how come I got a feather in the mail yesterday?*

---

* There was no return address on the envelope, but there was a note inside. It said, "No blame."